Wine Tides

Martin Ivanov

Published by Martin Ivanov, 2024.

This is a work of fiction. Similarities to real people, places, or events are entirely coincidental.

WINE TIDES

First edition. February 4, 2024.

ISBN: 979-8223501619

Written by Martin Ivanov.

1

My attention was captured by a blonde woman standing on the sidewalk, seemingly waiting for someone. She appeared to be no older than twenty-five. Her hair fell long, almost to her waist. She sported glasses and carried a red bag, looking around cautiously, gently removing her glasses and leaning slightly forward each time a car noise reached her ears.

I pulled up beside her. A faint dust arose from the stone streets under my tires. She recoiled, waving her hand as if to dismiss an irritating fly. A fine, gold-colored watch adorned her pale wrist.

"Excuse me, do you know where the White Dolphin hotel is?" I leaned on the window, trying to imitate a gangster film hero.

"A hotel?"

"I'm not sure. They said it was a hotel. Maybe it's some family house."

I surveyed her subtly, trying not to get caught. She wore fitting jeans and a reddish tank top. Her chest boldly outlined under the thin fabric of her top, stirring my imagination. Her breasts were quite large. I didn't mind if she caught me staring; I have a photographic memory - a blessing and a curse. I enjoyed etching such moments in my mind, storing them as a gallery of memories.

"I don't know of such a hotel," she said, her expression shifting from nervous to dismissive. "Sounds a bit low-end. Don't you have GPS? Just use it."

I knew where the hotel was. I was merely killing time and, more so, wanted to strike up a conversation with her. Unfortunately, she seemed arrogant, and my plan backfired. Her loss.

I remained there, gazing at her. She sensed my stare but pretended I was invisible. Treading the line between bold and rude, I rolled up the window and drove away.

I used to fear talking to women. Not anymore. After a few rejections, you become accustomed to it. Just think of something worse. It's like pain. When in pain, you yearn for pain elsewhere to overshadow the original one. It's the same with women's rejections. Most times, I thought about death. What's scarier than death? And if death is the ultimate fear, what's so bad about a woman's rejection? It's odd, but it helped me.

I drove on leisurely. It was too early to check into my hotel room, so there was no rush. Glancing in the side mirror, the blonde was rather ordinary. She resembled those cookie-cutter women, with identical eyebrows, lashes, lips, breasts, and so on. Not that I would've rejected her advances. And she seemed like a wine drinker. I'm fond of women who drink wine. Yet, she didn't strike me as one who could discern good wine from bad. But I could. When you drink a bottle, sometimes two a night, you learn. Good wine aids my writing; bad wine lulls me to sleep.

My sedan wasn't exactly built for speed. On the highway, I could hit a hundred kilometers per hour; in the city, barely thirty. Enough to irritate anyone tailing me. Luckily, there were few such drivers here. At the seaside, nobody hurries, especially not in the sweltering heat of July. I've noticed people become more relaxed the farther east you travel. But that's just my observation; I haven't been much to the West.

The seaside town's stone streets intertwined beautifully. I relished the view, although my sedan didn't quite share the sentiment. The sea unfolded beyond the old houses. The sunrise had passed, and the sun now drenched its rays into the water. I envied it. I longed for it.

Driving past the houses, I stopped in an alley with a sea view. Despite obstructing traffic, I lingered. Most drivers circumvented me silently. A few honked; I waved apologetically and continued my gaze.

My plan was a two-week stay, just enough to complete the novel I had begun. Started by choice, now loathed by obligation. I didn't want to write it anymore. But I had to.

2

I stopped in front of the "White Dolphin." Actually, the hotel was named "Blue Tide," as if tides could be any color but blue, but whatever. I don't know where I got that "White Dolphin" from. Probably why that blonde didn't recognize it either. She did have really nice, large breasts. For a moment, I imagined them hanging over me, although I'm more a fan of the smaller ones.

Forgive me, I am a man after all.

The hotel was actually quite small. I assumed the owners had a house here before and later converted it into a hotel. It had four floors and a huge yard. In the distance, I could see a pool in the yard, but it seemed to belong to the neighboring house or hotel, which was also for tourists, judging by the enormous signs above it. These people must be making good money during the summer season. And probably spending it somewhere in resorts during winter.

I got out of my sedan and with a bit more effort, managed to shut its door. Something inside clanked. It wasn't a usual sound, but it didn't matter. I expected any moment that this car would strand me and never start again. I turned to look at it. Aside from its light blue color starting to peel and fade, the car was dirty. If I managed to get away from it quickly enough, no one would realize it was mine. I planned to leave it here for the duration of my stay. I wasn't worried about someone stealing it. I actually wished it a new owner. This car deserved to be a model at a scrapyard.

The hotel's yard was accessible through a gate, and the gates were wide open. I strode in as if the hotel belonged to me. There, two people stopped their conversation and stared at me. Shorts, an unbuttoned shirt, unkempt hair, and unshaven. That's what they saw. The only thing missing from my appearance was a cigarette. And I missed it too. I had left them in the car.

At the reception worked an attractive lady. I always wondered if it was deliberate to have young and necessarily female staff at every reception. There were exceptions sometimes. Like last year, in another hotel, a boy worked there. He was skinny and tall. His arms were like sticks. He looked scared and barely responded. I hated talking to him. But now, standing in front of me was a dark-haired, young, and smiling woman. What more could one ask for in a receptionist? I approached her. Her hair smelled nice from afar. Her badge read Maria.

"Hello."

Adding to her smile, a lovely, feminine voice.

"I have a reservation."

"Your names?"

"Alexander Nik."

I was almost convinced that was the name I had used for the reservation. The girl asked for my ID card. After a short search, I found it in one of my pockets. She looked at the card, then at me, and then back at the card.

"Is there a problem?"

"Your ID says Alexander Diev."

"Just call me Alex," I smiled, a pathetic attempt to break the ice.

She smiled too. I liked her. She had small breasts hidden under her shirt. And she was short. I liked short girls, but only if they were naked. Otherwise, not really.

"Room 202." She handed back my ID, and her finger brushed against mine. Her hands were cold.

I don't boast, but women generally find me attractive. Not always, of course, but in most cases. I never understood what they saw in me, but it somehow worked.

She handed me a keychain with the key and a small tag marked 202. She smiled again. Women often hide a lot behind their smiles - lies, promises, temptations. And yet, I fell for it every time. Not the eyes, not the backside, not the breasts. The smile. And preferably with a full set of teeth.

The room wasn't anything special. For fifteen leva a night, it was more than satisfactory. A small corridor, a bathroom and toilet, and a larger room with a double bed. In front of the bed was a desk with a TV, which I doubted I would use. The unexpected thing was the balcony. Yes, it was small, but it had a table and two chairs. Enough for me to squeeze in there and write every night. I already pictured my laptop and a bottle of wine next to it, with the sea breeze hitting my face.

I stepped out onto the balcony. There was no view of the sea, but the view of the hotel across the street was good. On most of the balconies, towels were spread out. They seemed like women's. I hoped they were women's. In the big city, where there usually wasn't a sea, women didn't walk around in swimsuits on their balconies. But here they did. That's why I loved seaside resorts. Only half-naked women could be such a muse. Although I preferred them in my bed, not on opposite balconies.

I tossed my jacket onto the bed and lay down with my clothes on the covers.

Then I must have fallen asleep.

<h1 style="text-align:center">3</h1>

Lately, I had come to detest writing. It drove me to the brink of madness. Sometimes, I felt like deleting all my files and telling my agent I was going into farming. I'd herd sheep and cows, live in a barn, be smeared with dung, and have a wife weighing a hundred kilograms, but she'd never idolize any other man in her life except me.

It was evening. The attractive receptionist was gone, replaced by a larger one who also smiled. I had slept with such women over the years. As long as they smiled, that's all I wanted. I didn't like the sullen ones.

There was no one in the foyer of the reception. The two beige chairs were empty. Soft music played from somewhere. I left the key with the receptionist. She looked at me, trying to recall who I was. She couldn't, but still wished me a good evening.

The pool in the other yard was crowded. In the middle of July, even when the sun was setting, it was warm. However, most people were lounging on the sunbeds at the side, cocktails in hand, dressed in t-shirts and shorts.

My sedan was where I left it. Some guy leaned against it, resting his shoe on the tire. Honestly, it didn't annoy me. I pitied the guy more. He'd dirty his nice clothes. The lady he was talking to, standing upright in front of him, gave him a look I recognized. She would sleep with him tonight, no matter what he told her now.

Reluctantly, I opened the car door. My cigarettes were inside. The guy startled and quickly backed away.

"Sorry," he hurried to apologize.

"You can't harm this car anymore than it's already been." I waved him off without looking.

He chuckled but didn't lean on it again as I walked away. The girl also smiled at me but then looked back at the guy. He was the lucky one. Though if he wanted success with women, he should stay away from cars like mine. It didn't bring any luck. But the woman in front of him was already ready, I wonder if he realized that.

I went into the nearby supermarket and got cigarettes and wine. On my way to the checkout, I remembered I hadn't eaten anything. I went back for some salads and meat. Took some sweets too. They went well with the wine. I didn't need anything else. I stepped out of the supermarket and lit a cigarette. I wanted to enjoy the sun setting, turning into a reddish bomb, scattering its rays, painting everything in wine-red.

"How's your room?"

The voice was familiar. It was the girl from the reception, now dressed more nicely. She wore a wide skirt that reached above her knees, a tank top, and some sort of light denim jacket over it. In one hand, she held two bottles of alcoholic cider.

"The bed's great. Have you ever tried it?"

Her smile vanished. She looked at me sharply.

"I didn't mean it like that," I hastened to apologize. I never could learn that some people couldn't handle my humor.

"Got you," her smile returned. "I've slept on those beds."

"With clients, or?"

"You're pushing it, Alex... That was your name, right?"

I really was crossing the line, but I sensed she liked it. And she remembered my name. That was more interesting.

"Mr. Nik. Shouldn't everything be official?"

"By your ID, you're no Nik. And I'm not at work. I'm just a stranger in a supermarket parking lot."

"Ah, so we can have a cider? Maybe one of those in your hand?"

"Are you hitting on me?"

"Yes."

"You're too old for me."

She winked in that way that said "maybe" and walked away. She offered hope but kept her distance. I didn't mind. She got into a Mini Cooper and sped off. She wasn't driving. Another girl was at the wheel. I finished my cigarette and returned to the hotel. Her words, calling me old, stung a bit. But how much older could I be? I was about to turn 35, with two serious relationships behind me and having not seen a woman's body in over five months. Well, if I don't count the prostitute a few days ago. But I don't count the ones I pay for.

I returned to my hotel room. The plump woman at the reception smiled at me. She had a pretty face, but she was fat. I pushed the door and entered. The sun had almost disappeared. I ate quickly, set up my laptop on the balcony, stretched my legs on the chair in front of me, opened the wine, and gazed at the apartments across.

I started writing around midnight.

4

Writing came naturally to me, at least that's what the popularity of my first two books suggested. If you enter a library, you won't find my books in the bestseller section or among those of famous authors, but certainly, one of the saleswomen would recommend my books. Hopefully, they're good. A beautiful woman talking about books is the sexiest thing I could think of.

In one of my books, I wrote about a drunk actor; in the other, a drunk lawyer. The commonality between the two novels, apart from the inebriated protagonists, was romance and sex. People loved reading about sex. I don't know why. When I read books, I usually skipped those parts. Reading about others' passions left me feeling empty, as if I was seeking something I couldn't attain myself. I hoped someday someone would invent a way to visualize thoughts. An author could record the sex exactly as they imagined it in the book, and people like me could just watch it. If that ever gets invented, remember, I predicted it first.

The third book I was writing now was a bit banal. A boy likes a girl, the girl plays hard to get, and the boy starts doing foolish things. Only, both the girl's sister and mother fancy the boy, and each makes advances towards him. See, no alcohol. But there is sex. Old ladies who haven't found love in their lives will go crazy over it. My editor is optimistic, but my agent begs me not to write it. I told him I'd think about it, and here I am at the sea, having downed another bottle of wine, watching the sunrise, and having written ten more pages.

Ten pages were my daily minimum. I set it as a compulsory target and strictly adhered to it. After all, it brought in the money.

I had reached the part where the heroine tells the boy that it won't work between them and that she likes someone else. Naturally, it's much more nicely described in the book than how I'm telling you. Actually, this story is inspired by a friend's experience. The idea matured in my head and blossomed. Now, all that's left is to transfer it onto paper. Or rather, onto my laptop.

Morning had arrived, and I had been writing all night.

There was a knock at my door. I got up and went to open it, feeling slightly unsteady. An elderly woman stood there, dressed in a wide purple skirt with buttons, holding a bedsheet in her hand and looking at me strangely through her glasses.

"For a hundred, I expected someone younger," I couldn't help myself. The woman didn't know what to say. "But it's okay. You'll do. I've paid, after all."

I stepped back from the door and let her enter. But she remained on the threshold.

"Sir..." She was slightly frightened. "I... am here to change the beddings."

Of course, I knew that. I tried to joke, but apparently, I scared her. A family with two children passed behind her. The man was fat and tall, the woman shorter and much slimmer than him. Both glanced at me. And there I was, naked except for my shorts, and having not slept for over twenty-four hours. I must have looked pleasant to them. But the fat man's wife was not bad. Every such woman I saw gave me inspiration for a few more pages. That's how women affected me.

I sent the elderly housekeeper away. In movies, housekeepers were young, beautiful, and usually naked under their dresses. This one was probably just the latter. I shook my head at the thought. Most likely, as often happens, she would now tell her colleagues, and they would tell their boss, and they would tell the reception, and soon I'd get my first warning for eviction. It wouldn't be the first time.

I went into the bathroom, took a shower, smoked a cigarette on the balcony, and lay down to sleep. I fell asleep quickly. Like a boy who had just made love to the sister and mother of the girl he's in love with.

But that was only in my book.

5

I woke up in the early afternoon. My head didn't hurt, which meant the wine was good. But I was terribly hungry. I threw on some clothes and went out. I was hoping to see Maria at the reception, but it was the plump lady again. I handed her my room key.

"There was another girl here yesterday when I arrived," I couldn't resist asking.

"Strange. She asked about you too." Her eyes twinkled with amusement as she tried not to show it.

I smiled and backed away, watching her. The lady shyly averted her eyes. I wished her a pleasant evening. I felt like I was in a déjà vu.

My sedan was in its spot. I remembered the guy from yesterday. He must have scored. The sweetie he was talking to would have devoured him right on top of my car. I'm glad their first time together wasn't exactly on my sedan. Not for any particular reason, just that they would have gotten dirty.

I decided to treat myself that evening. I had slept enough, and my writing only started after midnight. And until then, there were many free hours. First, I went to the supermarket and grabbed something like a sandwich. Secretly, I was hoping to run into Maria, but I didn't. And she really was quite younger than me. I needed to get her out of my head.

I headed to the beach. I didn't want to swim. I planned to stroll along the shore, check out the ladies, sit on a bench, and smoke a cigarette. And that's exactly what I did.

I hadn't even smoked half the cigarette when I felt a gaze on me. On the next bench sat a blonde woman. She was tall and slim. Her hair was tied in a tight short ponytail, stretching her face. A little blonde boy, no more than three, ran around her. She alternated her gaze between the child and me. Her look wasn't one of the sexual kinds I had encountered before. It was more like fear. And while the first two times I thought it was a coincidence, the third time, I got up and went to her.

"Cigarette?"

A lame, yet effective move. Tradition. Long live cigarettes. They've brought so many families together. Well, they've also split quite a few.

"No, no. I don't smoke."

She recoiled as if I was offering her poison, which, in a sense, was true. I pointed to the empty seat next to her. Some guys wait for a hundred signals to be sure they can talk to a woman. But it's so obvious every time.

The first signal was her look, and the second was that she slightly withdrew and allowed me to sit. A look and decreasing distance. Did I need to wait for more signals?

"What's his name?"

"Peter."

"Nice name. My brother is called that."

I didn't have a brother. Or a sister. Just trying to open conversational doors.

"And what's your name?"

"Alexander," I extended my hand, and she gently shook it. I leaned in and kissed the top of her hand like in the movies. She liked that. I saw her smile. I love smiles.

"Alexander? How banal."

"Then call me whatever you want."

She laughed. The child, who was with her, ran around us.

"I noticed you were looking at me."

"Me? You're mistaken."

"If I were mistaken, you wouldn't have let me sit. And why are we talking so formally?"

She smiled and glanced away for a moment.

"Actually, I was looking at you. You seemed interesting. Is that not allowed?"

"I've been told before that I'm interesting. But mostly in a bad way. Sometimes I look like a sick man, other times a homeless one."

"I think you're a writer."

Damn, she was good.

"What gave me away?"

"The dreamy look."

"How do you know I'm not thinking about an ex?"

"If you were sixteen, maybe I would think that. But you seem a bit older."

"Just a bit," I affirmed, trying to maintain a serious tone. She smiled.

"What do you write about?"

"I won't tell. I'm superstitious. And if I tell you, you'll take your child and leave."

"It's not my child. It's my sister's."

I won't lie, that reassured me a bit. I've been with young mothers twice before. Not that it's bad, but instead of cuddling after sex, they got up and ran to their child.

"And it seems you've experienced this before."

God, this stranger was reading my face. Cynic, drunkard, writer. What else did she see in me?

"But you seem like a good catch," she continued.

"A good catch?"

"We had a nice conversation."

"Shall we continue somewhere else?"

I felt I was losing her, so I got more direct. The blonde woman smiled at me and stood up. She called the boy by name a few times, and he finally came. She dressed him, and he sat between us, looking at a toy in his hands. He would grow up to be handsome. Certainly better looking than me.

"Tomorrow, same time, here again. Bring flowers."

She took the child by the hand and turned her back on me. She had a nice butt. I liked such women. Not for the butt, but for her direct approach. I had some need to be controlled. When I took matters into my own hands, I usually dropped them. She wanted a second meeting and flowers.

"What's your name?" I called after them, but she didn't hear. Only little Peter turned and said his name again.

6

I returned to the hotel with a new bottle of wine and some food. The plump woman was apparently pulling another night shift at the reception.

"Seems I keep missing your colleague?"

"She's here from 7 in the morning to the afternoon. Then it's me."

"So, we won't be seeing each other anymore?"

"If it's that urgent, should we swap shifts?" She teased me with her gaze.

"No, no need. Just joking. What's your name?"

I asked, even though I had already seen her badge.

"Miroslava. Nice to meet you."

"Alexander. But you probably already know."

"Yes. I saw it earlier when you were leaving. But I didn't understand how long you'll be staying?"

"If everything is alright, two weeks."

"If everything is alright? Is there something you're unhappy with? The beddings, the TV...?"

Oh God, I hope she hadn't heard about the incident with the housekeeper this morning.

"No, my room is great. I meant something else."

"Ah, sorry." she said and handed me the keys.

I tapped lightly on the counter with my knuckles and went upstairs. A woman was coming down the stairs. She wore a swimsuit under some kind of satin cape, shimmering in the light as if straight out of a high fashion magazine. Our eyes met and didn't part until our bodies did. Wow, this woman was fire.

And she smelled of lavender. She was the fat man's wife I saw earlier.

Could her husband satisfy her enough? Doubtful. Probably he lay on his stomach, his body spreading across the bed, she climbed on top of him, and everything was over in two to three minutes. I had slept with many dissatisfied wives. They detailed their love lives for me. It didn't take much to read her gaze. Yes, maybe she saw "something interesting" in me and not the man of her dreams. But her look showed a lack of sex. Don't ask me how I know, I can't explain. You learn it by looking at the right place. Not in the cleavage or trembling butts, but in the eyes.

My room was the second-to-last in the corridor. From the last one, I heard a child's voice. The fat man's wife must be living there with him. What a picture that painted. Black short hair gently touching her shoulders, blue eyes ready to wreck even the most exemplary man's life.

I lay playing with my phone, waiting for it to get dark. That's when I liked to write, when my muse arrived. Until then, I poured myself a glass of wine and ate something quickly. My eating habits were terrible, but I was an artist, at least that's how people labeled me. So, my body was the least of my concerns. My phone rang.

"Hello, Alex?"

I recognized the voice. It was Denis, my agent.

"Where are you?"

"At the seaside."

"The seaside? Weren't you writing a book?"

"That's why I'm here."

"That book?"

"Yes. Finishing it."

"Listen, we have an offer for a series."

"You've got the wrong number, bro. I'm not an actor."

"Shut up and listen, you hopeless writer."

Denis often exploded and then apologized. That was his style. Quick to ignite and quick to cool. At first, it annoyed me, but now it just made me laugh.

"I'm listening!" I replied dutifully.

"The book about the drunk actor."

"Fifty Milliliters of a Role?"

"The same trash. Like the rest of your books."

I was already laughing out loud.

"Listen, there's interest in a series based on the book. They want a sample script from you by the end of the month."

"What script from me? I already gave them a whole book."

"Better write it yourself, hear me. That way you'll have control. Otherwise, they'll write it and ruin your book."

"How much worse can it get?"

"That's what I asked them." Now he was laughing. "But jokes aside, the money is really good."

"How much?"

"With my 10% or without?"

"How much are they offering? Stop messing with me."

"10 thousand to write the script."

"That's not much."

"You've never seen that much money at once, you silly writer."

"That's true. Anything extra?"

"If they like it and the series takes off, there'll be bonuses. But you have to be involved in the making."

I pondered. I had never been involved in making a series. An interesting prospect was on the horizon. For a moment, I even imagined myself there. Sitting on a chair with my name embroidered on it, wearing black glasses, biting a cigarette, and glaring at the actors.

"Hello, Alex? Hello..."

"I'm here. Just thinking."

"So, you accept?"

"I haven't said anything yet."

"You don't have much choice. I accepted on your behalf."

"How..."

"We'll talk. I don't mind your new book anymore. From what I hear, it's a good plot for a porn film. And if they contact us from there, I'll be swimming in yachts thanks to your perverted imagination."

The call ended. I was going to accept. I liked the offer as soon as I heard it, but it annoyed me when someone did things over my head. Write a script. It sounded interesting. For some reason, I thought of the plump receptionist, Mira. Would she say, "I know him, he stayed at our hotel," when she read my name in the film credits and saw my face in interviews?

7

I wrote again until the early morning, reaching the first hints of the girl's mother flirting with the boy who liked her daughter. It sounds confusing when I say it, but believe me, it's turning out great. Especially for those looking for such plots. My first two books were about alcohol, the third about sex. Some great poets and writers would turn in their graves if they knew what I write. But what does it matter, as if they never thought about the same while writing their love letters.

This time, I wrote twelve pages, two more than my target. I felt proud and was making good progress. My writing productivity increased proportionally to the number of women's behinds in swimsuits I saw. If they were naked, I'd give even more of myself. But for now, luck wasn't smiling at me. Though, it seemed like that could change.

This time, I let the housekeeper clean. My bed needed freshening up. I bit a cigarette in my mouth and started helping her without being asked. Usually, housekeepers are displeased in such situations and insist on doing it themselves, but this one just thanked me. Would she have still thanked me if I had lit the cigarette? Doubtful.

When she left, I thanked her and wished her an easy evening. She gave me a strange look, and I felt foolish for saying it. But for me, it was evening. I was about to sink into the realm of dreams. Moreover, the weather today looked rainy and bad. Perfect for sleep.

I brought my laptop in from the balcony and left the door wide open. I needed the fresh air from outside to cleanse everything bad around me. From the next room, I heard shouting. The fat man and his wife were arguing. I fell asleep listening to them. The black-haired woman with blue eyes was under my covers. She kissed my knees, then my thighs. Then I felt her tongue where I wanted it most. One hand was around my 'staff of love', the other stretched forward and placed on my stomach. Just as I approached the sublime moment, I woke up.

It was just before 3 PM. It was bright outside but slightly cool. The rain had brought the temperatures down, making them pleasant for July. The wine bottle on the bedside table was half-empty. I was ashamed; I hadn't even managed to finish it. But at least I had written a lot that night. Then I remembered the argument between the fat man and his wife. She shouted with a very sweet voice. But unfortunately, it was muffled, and I couldn't hear what they were arguing about. Then I dreamt of her. I hadn't actually seen that she was the woman in my dream, but I was sure of it. That's how dreams work. You're given information, even if you don't see it.

The shower I took invigorated me. I emerged slowly from the bathroom and sat on the bed. I had slept over eight hours but felt beaten up. Should I stop drinking, or was my body just struggling to adjust to the seaside climate? I sat on the bed and buried my face in my hands. I was missing something. There was a void. Something I needed to do but hadn't. I had written enough, drunk, bathed, and dreamt of my neighbor without knowing her. Well, the last one wasn't on my daily to-do list, but I was glad it happened.

But I had forgotten about the meeting with the blonde woman and her child from yesterday.

I felt awful. I put on the first clean clothes I found, threw the wet towel on the bed, and almost ran out. It was just after 3:30 PM. In the worst case, I would be a few minutes late. I walked quickly, glad that it wasn't as hot as the previous days. The rain had washed the streets and refreshed the town. There was almost no one on the beach, and the waves were big, crashing against the rocks.

As I approached, I slowed down, put my hands in my pockets, bit an unlit cigarette, and unbuttoned the top button of my shirt. I started to regret coming out in just a shirt, as it was quite cold.

I forgot about the cold when I saw her.

She stood under the tree where the bench was but hadn't sat down. The bench was wet. She was wearing a long summer dress with various patterns. Her neckline was open, though she didn't have very large breasts. Now that she stood straight, her neck looked longer, and her cheekbones gave her face a sharper look that I couldn't describe, even though I considered myself a writer. She was smiling. I loved smiling people.

"I had already thought you wouldn't come."

I decided to preempt her by saying it first. That definitely surprised her.

"Very funny. Making a lady wait in the rain. And where are my flowers?"

If only she knew I had even forgotten her, let alone the flowers.

"They got soaked in the rain and didn't survive to meet you."

"I've never heard of rain killing flowers."

Of course, she didn't believe me. Especially with such pathetic excuses as mine.

"Oh, I know many stories about dead flowers."

She looked at me strangely. For a moment, I saw doubt in her eyes. It wasn't something I hadn't seen before. I often exaggerated; I knew it. It wasn't just sometimes. I exaggerated almost always. But with me, you had a chance only if you accepted me as I am. There was no getting used to it. I learned that from my two longer relationships. Both women had accepted me as I was. And when they stopped liking it, they left me. Well, that and a few affairs with other women. But those were mistakes, not part of my character.

She was dressed nicely and smelled good. And I thanked myself for at least having showered. I hoped I didn't still reek of wine. Really, what did these women see in me?

We walked along the alley. She was tall, slim, blonde, and beautiful. And I was unkempt, dark-haired, and moderately ugly. But at least I was taller than her. Most people we passed looked at us. Well, they looked at her. They probably cursed me and wondered what she saw in me. Just like I wondered about the fat man and his wife in the next hotel room.

"I haven't seen you around here; are you a tourist?"

"Let's say yes."

"Let's say?"

"I travel a lot. I find it hard to stay in one place. Most of my baggage is in the car."

"Must be a very big car."

"Better not to see it. And how much is a man's luggage? Two or three t-shirts, a couple of jeans, and lots of socks and underwear. At least one for every day of the week."

"That's a lot. I've met guys who don't even change their underwear every day."

"How many of those have you dated?"

"Are we going to talk about my exes' underwear? Not very romantic."

"I'm not particularly jealous."

"You're not jealous, and you want to talk about men's underwear."

"Maybe you're right."

It was the strangest conversation I've had with a woman. But my rebellious mouth sometimes embarrassed me. Sometimes we didn't get along. I preferred writing to talking.

"Aren't you going to ask something about me?"

I wasn't particularly interested. I just wanted to get her into bed.

"Where are you from?"

"Here."

"Here?" That intrigued me. "A local?"

"Something like that."

"But you have houses or?"

"Three houses. Two are converted into rental rooms for tourists. In the third, I live with my mother, my sister, and her child."

"That's why you don't have a man."

"Why?"

"Well, most men here are just for the summer. And if you trap one, he'd have to live with your mother."

"What's wrong with my mother?"

"I assume she's a very nice woman, but how do you imagine a serious man agreeing to live with his wife's mother?"

She fell silent. I didn't know if she was pondering or if I had offended her again. It would be a miracle if she could stand me until the end of our meeting.

"I live well enough without a man."

"I believe you."

I didn't believe her.

"Do you drink wine?"

She stopped and turned to me. I tried to be as serious as I could.

"Wine? What kind of question is that?"

"I'm a connoisseur of wine."

"A connoisseur or a drunkard?"

"Maybe I shouldn't have asked."

She laughed.

"What are you writing about now?"

"I haven't confirmed that I'm a writer. You just assumed."

"You're a writer. It's written all over your face. I've been with writers. Actually, just once. Always dreamy, lost in thoughts, and far from reality. You're the same. I can tell by your look."

"And yet you went out with me?"

"No. You went out with me. If it were up to you, you would have slept with me yesterday and not recognized me today."

"I'm still up for that."

She tried to hide her smile, but I caught it.

"Yes, you're a writer. And you constantly write about sex. You have your characters make love at every possible moment. And when you can't do that, you just get them drunk."

I wouldn't exaggerate by saying that for the first time, a woman had left me astounded like that. I was now suspecting she had quite a rich experience with men. Everything she said was true, even though I didn't see it. When someone tells you the truth you've managed to hide even from yourself, it hurts. But that's how I made money and my books sold. Was I just trying to justify myself?

And then silence fell between us. She gave me time to respond.

"Actually, you're somewhat right."

"Somewhat?"

"I write about sex."

"I knew it," her smile was beautiful. But I had noticed that yesterday too.

"But it sells."

"Yes. But there's also romance without sex."

"You can't convince me of that."

"It's much more beautiful to read about the thoughts and feelings of a person in love than about where and how many times they've had sex."

"Wait, wait," Now I stopped. "I don't write for the porn industry."

I must have said it too loudly because an old lady nearby turned and looked at us disapprovingly. The beauty I was with, whose name I still didn't know, blushed a bit but also laughed quietly.

"Are you going to take me somewhere, or are we just going to walk around?"

"You tell me. I'm new here, you're a local."

"I know a very nice place. But first, ask me my name."

"Your name is probably something short. No more than four letters."

"Olga. How did you guess?"

"Lucky guess. Is it Russian?"

"My father was Russian. He owned these properties here. But he died two years ago."

"I'm sorry. But at least he left you properties."

"I like you, but sometimes you're terrible."

"The motto of my life."

<h1 style="text-align:center">8</h1>

Olga led me through a quiet and narrow street. If everyone hadn't been staring at us as they passed, I might have thought she was trying to kidnap me. But what use was I to her? A poor writer, a drunkard, driving an old car that could fall apart at any moment, barely making it to my vacation. I wouldn't even be good for some illegal organ transplant scheme unless she wanted to torture me for fun. But after so much alcohol over the years, I doubted I'd feel any pain she might want to inflict.

We stopped in front of a gate under large trees. Olga pushed the small door; it creaked slightly as we entered. The yard wasn't big, and the house looked a bit old from the outside, but the lights around it and the flowers everywhere made it somehow beautiful.

"Bringing me to your place before we've even got to know each other?"

She put her hand over my mouth and pointed to a small path beside the house. I followed it like an obedient puppy. I didn't need a second invitation. Olga removed her shoes and entered the house. I circled around and found myself in a yard on the side of the house.

There, on a well-mowed lawn, was a gazebo, and next to it, a swing. The swing would have been too cheesy, so I sat in the gazebo. A few lights on the first floor of the house turned on and then off. Olga must have passed there. A motorcycle sounded in the street. And when the sound faded away, Olga came out of the house and headed towards me. She was barefoot. In one hand, she held a bottle of wine, in the other, two glasses. A beautiful woman with wine. I loved such sights. But I wasn't sure if I was happier to see her or the wine.

"I expected you to be sitting on the swing."

"I thought it would be too gay."

"Now I'm sure you only write about sex. There's not a gram of romance in you."

She was wrong. In the novel I was writing, there was romance. The sister and mother of the girl that the boy likes, their romance towards him. It's incredibly confusing. And she wants me to tell her what I write about. Even explaining it to myself was difficult.

Olga sat on the swing, crossed her legs one over the other, and poured wine into one glass. She left the other empty. This slightly annoyed me. Not because she was drinking without me, although that irritated me too, but because she would win this mini-game. But that's how women are. Once they set their mind on something, that's it.

"My first book was about a drunken actor." I started. Although my first book enjoyed good success, I was still embarrassed to talk about it. I preferred to stop there. I wasn't interested in what people thought about my books. I just wanted them to buy them and be quiet.

"Typical."

I pretended not to hear her.

"The second is about a drunken lawyer."

Now she laughed. I expected that.

"Let me guess. The one you're writing now is about a drunken pilot."

"No. It's about a Russian woman who meets a random man and takes him home the same evening."

"That's not our first night, and if you think we're doing anything more than drying up this bottle, you better leave now. And I'm not Russian."

I left the glass next to her and stood up. I wished her a good evening, and she did the same. I walked down the path I had come. I was bluffing. In a moment, I'd return like an obedient puppy.

"Yes, I love wine."

Her soft voice made me turn around.

"Didn't you ask me earlier? I love wine. But I don't like drinking it alone."

I went back to her. I poured my glass almost to the brim and tried to drink it slowly, unlike my usual habit. We talked about life by the sea, living with her mother. I learned her sister had been abandoned by her husband and was raising the child alone. Olga helped when needed, but it affected her personal life. I also found out that the house we were at was one of those rented to tourists and was empty tonight, but they were expecting a group tomorrow. I learned she grew up here and had never been to Russia but wanted to see her grandparents there. She found out my age, and I learned hers. She was twenty-six, nine years younger than me. And she made it clear she wasn't looking for anything serious. I wasn't either, but I was dying to sleep with her. Even now, I wanted to grab her tied hair and kiss her neck. Was I asking for too much?

Olga went for a second bottle. When she disappeared around the corner, I followed her. She entered the house, and I went in after her.

9

Someone was shouting outside, probably drunk. Maybe that's why Olga hadn't heard me when I followed her inside. But she was expecting me. I entered the room, and she was bending over into the fridge, pulling out a new bottle. Then she felt my presence and froze. She put down the bottle, and I was already close to her. She turned to face me, leaning her back against the kitchen counter, stretched out her arms, and grabbed my face. And I buried mine in hers.

With one hand, I bared her right thigh, slipped my hand under it, and lifted her onto the counter. The wine bottle fell into the sink but remained intact. We could finish it later. But first, I wanted to drink everything from her. She moaned in ecstasy.

And I hadn't even penetrated her yet. She wanted me. I wanted her too. Very much. I lifted her other leg. Olga looked like a woman in a gynecologist's chair, waiting for the doctor to insert something into her most sacred spot.

And I was the doctor.

My belt was already on the floor, jeans pulled down. I didn't remember doing it. Probably her doing. I felt her saliva in my mouth all the while. She kissed me so passionately that I momentarily feared for my tongue. Something broke behind me. It was one of the glasses. I didn't care. Neither did she, even more so.

She moaned a second time. This time louder.

And this time I was inside her. And on the second thrust, she climaxed. So did I. I heard a soft laugh on my shoulder.

"I don't even know you."

She was feeling guilty. But despite that, she had relaxed into me and was breathing heavily.

"We know each other's names." My breath was also shaky. I kissed her on the chin.

"I'm a writer, and you're a local."

I kissed her again, this time on the nose.

"I'm thirty-five, and you're twenty-six."

I kissed her lower lip. She tilted her face up.

"We drank wine together."

She wrapped her arms around me. If her arms weren't so weak, she would have strangled me, so tightly she clung to me. I wrapped my arms around her waist and carried her across the room. I'm not sure, but I think I was still inside her the entire journey.

"To the right." She gently guided me.

We entered a dark room. Olga reached out and turned on the light.

In the middle of the room was a double bed, covered with a fluffy duvet and neatly arranged fluffy pillows. Among them were plush toys. The long, red curtains hung from the windows. The lamp cast one of those quiet white lights that made the room simultaneously bright and slightly gloomy. I let her fall back onto the bed. As she fell, she looked into my eyes. She looked at me lovingly. That was the only thing I didn't like. I hadn't come here to fall in love.

I climbed on top of her. Ready for a second time to penetrate. And I did. She arched her neck and dug her nails into my back. With each thrust, her nails dug deeper. I felt blood trickling down my back, running sideways, and dripping onto her duvet. On the last thrust, she screamed. I did too, but mine was muffled by her.

I lay down next to her. She was still in her dress, and I was in socks and a t-shirt. We didn't speak. Each of us stared at a different spot on the ceiling. Blood spots were on her hands. My back was stinging terribly. But the pleasure I had felt twice in just the last ten minutes overshadowed the pain.

"I think we made a bit of a mess."

She turned to look at me. She bared her white teeth and smiled. I think she hadn't heard what I said.

She leaned over me, put her palms on my shoulders, propped herself up on them, and climbed on top of me. She took off her dress. Her nipples were erect, standing beautifully on her small breasts. I sat up and sucked on one. She moaned again, looking at the ceiling. I moved to the other. The reaction was the same.

My t-shirt was also now somewhere on the floor. Olga wiped her bloody hands on my chest and started kissing me. I was inside her for the third time. I hoped it would last longer this time.

She wasn't the most beautiful I had been with, but she was one of the most passionate. Just her moans drove me to the edge. I felt like we could do it a hundred times in one night, and I wouldn't last more than a minute each time. At least for now, we were even – two for two.

Olga leaned forward onto me. Again she moaned. This time, so did I.

I wrapped my arms around her backside and pulled her towards me. She put her hands on my chest and squeezed them, then began to thrust a little more roughly back and forth. She removed my hands from her backside, intertwined her fingers with mine, stretched them back, and lay on me stomach-down, bending her knees.

"No." I gasped. "Give me a chance..."

She laughed and looked into my eyes. Those hazel eyes finished me. I climaxed for the third time. But she didn't. I was disappointed, but then I saw her look. She was thanking me with her eyes.

"We didn't finish the second bottle."

Even now, I was trying to be witty. I could have just leaned over to her and put my tongue in her mouth.

She laughed and did what I regretted not doing.

I grabbed her hair and sucked her lips again.

10

We did it two more times until morning. On the last try, I managed to last about five minutes, which I consider an achievement. In the end, it wasn't about how long it lasted but the pleasure we gave each other. The damp duvet, soaked with blood, lipstick, and sweat, bore witness to the passion that had consumed the room.

Olga fell asleep on my shoulder, naked. I threw whatever I could find over her. We were too exhausted to even think about heading to the bathroom. I checked my watch. Barely an hour had passed, but it felt like an entire evening. Shortly after, I fell asleep too.

I woke up before her, shivering. The window was open, and the morning was chilly. Olga hadn't moved all night. Clothes were scattered around, the fluffy duvet was in tatters, and there were blood stains on Olga's body – from my back. And the wounds there must have been deep because they not only stung but also pulsed.

First, I checked if she was breathing. I had never experienced anything like it, but I had heard stories and didn't think it would happen to me. Olga was breathing, but clearly very tired. She didn't even feel me moving her arm and getting up. I tried to find the bathroom but failed. I passed through the kitchen. The wine bottle was still in the sink, and a broken glass lay on the floor. I cleaned up what I could and returned to the bedroom. Looking at Olga, I doubted she'd wake up soon. I gathered my clothes, dressed, and left.

Outside, it was bright. Usually, I greeted the first rays of sun half-drunk and content with what I had written during the night. Now, I faced them sober and dissatisfied with my writing, but pleased with life. My shirt was crumpled but definitely cleaner than my body. My jeans were wrinkled.

I walked through the streets like a drunk, despite not having touched alcohol. My thoughts were on Olga. There are people with whom you connect in character but not in bed. With others, only the sex works. With her, we had plenty to talk about, and it felt like we were two puzzle pieces meant to fit into each other. But I knew such things happened at the seaside and doubted we'd see each other again. Though I was sure I would miss her.

I entered my hotel. It was just past seven. The foyer was empty, but at the reception desk was not the plump woman but Maria.

"Someone partied all night," her lips thin and wide.

"Highly unprofessional to say to a hotel guest," I tried to sound serious.

"I'm sorry, Mr. Nik, I..."

"I'm joking," I laughed. "But you fell for it."

"Yes." She looked relieved. "What happened to your hand?"

I looked at my hand. It was covered in blood. I smiled, and Maria blushed.

"I see, a third unprofessional comment."

"You learn fast. You'll make a good receptionist."

"With such meticulous guests at the hotel, how can I not?"

"Now, if you'll excuse me, I'd like to go to my room."

"The cleaners will be there any minute. You might want to wait."

"No. Better they don't enter. I need some rest."

"You don't look drunk."

"I don't drink much." I winked at her.

"Empty wine bottles in your room say otherwise."

That startled me a bit.

"Third unprofessional statement. Have you been in my room?"

"Not me, but the cleaners..."

"Isn't that client confidentiality or something?"

Maria guiltily looked down at her desk.

"Relax, I'm joking." I wasn't, but I genuinely didn't mind her. "If you want, come up and check out the bottles. Maybe we can finish one if any's left."

Maria looked around as if we were discussing something secretive.

"I'm working, I can't go up to rooms."

"After work?"

She frowned. That was enough for me to stop probing. I took my keys and went upstairs. Neither the duvet was changed nor the bottles thrown away. She had lied. Cleaners hadn't been in here, or maybe one of them had.

I needed a quick nap. I woke up just after twelve.

Someone was knocking on my door.

11

I opened the door and saw the maid again, yet her attention was not on me but directed towards someone in the corridor, who was loudly berating her:

"Did the door say not to enter?"

"Yes, sir."

"Then why did you?"

"I got confused."

"Confused, huh? You have no idea how confused I can make you."

"No, please."

Stepping forward, I saw a large man confronting me, the husband of the woman I had met on the stairs, identifiable by the scent of lavender. Shirtless, with a thick necklace dangling from his neck and wearing shorts that resembled swimwear more than anything, he presented a daunting figure.

"What seems to be the problem?" I asked, aiming for a friendly tone.

"Get back inside. Why are you meddling?"

I'm not fond of confrontations, but I dislike being spoken to in such a manner even more.

"You're shouting outside my room."

"If you want, I can shout inside your room. Close the door, or I'll force you inside."

"I doubt you could fit through the door."

Enraged, the man charged at me. The elderly maid attempted to intercept him but failed. I underestimated him; he managed to get through the door. In a few steps, I was on the bed, defensively eyeing his next move. The scene must have looked ridiculous from any outsider's perspective. Me, half-naked and standing on the bed, and him, also half-dressed, standing by the bed, eyes wide open. It was as if we were in a standoff seen in western movies, each moment away from drawing guns. Except there were no guns, and I was significantly lighter than him. If he attacked, I had nowhere to run. He would overpower me. Luckily, he gestured dismissively, cursed, and backed away.

"The hell with you and that stupid maid."

He stormed off to his room, slamming the door behind him.

"What happened?" I inquired of the maid.

"He was shouting and yelling into the phone."

"That's it?"

"Yes. I didn't hear him and entered. His eyes were red when he saw me..."

"It's alright, you can come in."

I allowed her in to change the sheets. I asked if she had come in yesterday, and she said she hadn't. That was all I needed to know. It must have been Maria or someone else from the staff. But why? And what if I had been inside? The situation was beginning to worry me, though I wouldn't mind if, while I slept, she climbed on top of me as Olga did the previous night. I regretted not taking Olga's number. Maybe we could've met again.

I turned on my laptop and moved it to the terrace. It was already sweltering outside. I opened the file with my book. I tried to write, but couldn't. I can't write during the day, and the evening had been lost to primal instincts. But I had no regrets.

I received an email from my agent, Denis. He had sent information about the screenplay for a series. Before opening it, I calculated the bonuses promised through it. If all went well, I'd earn enough to live comfortably for at least three more years without earning another lev. It was a good offer. They wanted the script by the end of the month, but I would be here for the next two weeks and somewhere else for the last. And I still had more of the book to write. I was nowhere close to being done.

There was a knock on my door. I felt like I was in a sitcom about neighbors where something was always happening. Opening it, there she was. The blue-eyed, black-haired beauty. Smelling of lavender, again.

"May I come in?"

How could she not? We might even lay down. Spend an unforgettable evening together.

"Yes." I tried to keep my voice calm and stepped back to let her in.

12

I had completely forgotten about the empty wine bottles and the food wrappers from my quick meals, catching myself in a moment of embarrassment. In the blue eyes of the woman standing before me, I must have seemed like a drunkard causing trouble. And to make matters worse, I still had blood on my hands, which I hastily hid behind my back.

"Hello, my name is Lora."

Lora? The name suited her.

"I'm sorry for barging in like this, but I didn't want my husband to see me talking to you."

"And your husband is?" I feigned ignorance, though I knew very well who he was.

"The hefty gentleman you had an altercation with earlier."

"Oh, yes. No problem. We sorted it out."

"He's not usually troublesome."

"No one is born bad."

"No, he's not bad. Just the maid surprised him..."

"I spoke with her. She said she made a mistake."

"Yes. I also spoke with her. Everything is fine now."

"You're lying."

"Not at all. Really..."

"How can anyone be fine after being looked at with those beautiful eyes?"

"Please..."

Though she first gave me a strange look, Lora then turned her gaze to the wall, where there was nothing. She had blushed, a clear sign she had taken a liking to the compliment. Now came the next step: either she would deny it or pretend to be angry.

"Did I say something wrong?"

"No... Actually, yes. My husband is just through that wall."

"But he doesn't know you're here."

"Are you blackmailing me?"

"No, of course not. I was just giving you a compliment. That's all. I bet that fatso hasn't given you one in a while."

"Fatso?"

She slapped me.

I won't lie; I liked it. I smiled, and she reached to slap me again, but I caught her hand.

"Is that blood?"

Showing her my hand was a mistake.

"No, it's from the wine."

"What am I even doing? Apologizing to a drunkard. I'm leaving. My husband was probably right about you."

"I'm not a drunkard. I'm a writer."

As soon as I said it, I realized how ridiculous it sounded. Lora turned around, raising her eyebrows questioningly. It didn't matter to her. She reached the door and turned back.

"What do you write?"

"A love story."

I wasn't lying. It was almost a love story.

"What's it about?"

"The usual. A boy loves a girl, the girl doesn't like the boy, and the boy ends up sleeping with her sister. Maybe even her mother."

Her eyes widened. I smiled and lit a cigarette, hoping the smoke wouldn't reach the ceiling sensors. Lora watched me for a few seconds before bursting into laughter so loud she had to cover her mouth to keep the sound from reaching the next room, where her husband was.

"I want to read it."

"It's not finished yet."

She approached my desk, where my laptop was open, clicked to compose a new email, and sent a blank one to herself. Sitting back, she looked up at me with her blue eyes, directly into mine. What did these women see in me?

"That's my email. I want you to send me part of your novel."

"I have other books. You can buy any of those."

"Do they have sex in them?"

"Yes, but not as much as this one."

"I want to be the first to read this one. Before you even publish it."

"And if I don't?"

"I'll tell the fatso you forced me in here."

"Fatso?"

She laughed and quietly exited the room.

13

In the afternoon, I decided to head to the beach. Just me, a couple of beers, some bare behinds, and lounging in the shade. I wasn't particularly fond of getting into the water. Generally, I didn't much care for sand either.

I found my swim shorts, a red pair with palm trees printed on them. I've had them for over five years but wore them no more than ten times. To my delight, they still fit. I debated whether to take my phone with me. I wanted to go and just watch the waves, to rest. In the end, I decided to bring it along. Lacking a towel, I took one from the hotel. The maid was now in my corner, so she wouldn't mind.

At the reception was the stout Miroslava. I greeted her, but she didn't notice me. The foyer was busy with people checking in. I tried to scan the crowd but found nothing of interest. Most were elderly. The group was not small.

Exiting the hotel, I noticed the neighboring pool was crowded again. The music had been turned down; they tried to keep it off in the afternoon so guests could rest in their rooms. By 5 PM, it would be back on. Passing my sedan, I felt a mix of relief and disappointment each time I saw it, half-hoping someone would steal it. That way, I'd at least know someone wanted it more than me. But I'd likely just end up fined for leaving my "junk" in a public space.

Walking under the trees, the weather was pleasant. However, the sun was scorching. Thankfully, the beach was close, so I didn't have to walk far. Approaching the sand, I glanced at the bench where I had met Olga. Now, another mother was there, with a little girl running around her. I thought about introducing myself, but luck like with Olga comes once. More likely, the child's father would appear and end my miserable existence.

The first steps on the sand were challenging. It had heated up and burned my soles. Some youths played volleyball, three overweight men argued loudly with beers in hand, umbrellas everywhere, elderly women topless, young ones running along the shore, ensuring all eyes were on their sculpted behinds. Men played cards, others read books. Women hid behind sunglasses, secretly hoping someone would come and talk to them. Nothing unusual or unseen. I couldn't understand the fascination with beach life, though I was here for the air, especially the morning air when everyone else was still asleep.

I bypassed the paid spots and found a free area, laying down my hotel towel. My neighbors were absent, but their umbrella cast a nice shadow, which I decided to share. I settled down, enduring the slight sting from the wounds Olga had given me on my back before relaxing.

To my right was an elderly couple. The grandmother was topless, her enormous breasts mercilessly pulled down by gravity. She read a book, occasionally looking up to catch any interesting happenings. The grandfather sat on his towel, eyeing the young behinds, likely dreaming of touching one more time in his life. I wasn't sure if that was his wish, but it's what I would be thinking in his shoes.

I lay there, seeking interesting sights. Two women, one older and the other younger, approached from the sea directly towards the towels in front of me. The older one was about fifty, with curly hair and slight wrinkles, wearing glasses. A blue swimsuit contained her large breasts. The younger one, possibly around twenty, might not have been her daughter but was taller, with a long face, wide lips, and brown eyes matching her hair color. The younger woman paid me no mind, but the older one approached.

"Excuse me, but we'll need to move the umbrella towards us."

I pretended not to notice them initially, then slightly raised myself.

"Should I move closer too?"

"No, thank you. We can manage without you."

She rotated her umbrella, and my shade disappeared. I stayed put, not in the mood to move. I didn't plan on staying long anyway.

The older woman bent over to adjust her umbrella, and for a moment, her privates nearly came into full view right in front of me. I felt like a teenager seeing the opposite sex's genitals for the first time, thrilled just like one.

I had fallen asleep.

Warm female hands touched my shoulder. For a moment, from the touch, I thought it was Lora, my neighbor from the hotel. But then I woke up and saw one of the women kneeling beside me, shouting something.

"Sir..."

It was the older woman. Calling her "old" seemed almost an insult to me too. She gently pressed my shoulder. I was awake now but pretended not to be. Then I felt the pain.

"Sir..."

I sat up. The front of my body was in agony.

"We're leaving now."

"That's a pity."

"Do you want us to leave the umbrella? The sun will burn you."

I touched my chest. It was already burning.

"I'm afraid it's a bit late for that."

"I have some sunscreen. If you want, you can still apply it."

"Only if you help me."

I had forgotten about the younger woman. She stood aside, arms crossed, disapproving of the scene.

"I'm trying to help you, but you're acting like an idiot."

"My therapist says the same. You must be right."

I sat up, and her breasts were just a meter in front of my eyes. I could bury my head in them right then. No, I wasn't crazy enough to do such a thing. But what's wrong with people expressing their sexual impulses wherever they feel like it? I thought it would make for a very healthy and fulfilled society.

The woman took out a white bottle from her bag and handed it to me. I put out my hands, and she sprayed some into them. She stood up. The view from below was equally pleasant. I applied the sunscreen on my chest without much effort.

"Where can I return the umbrella to you?"

"Where are you staying?"

"Surf, Breeze... honestly, I don't remember the name."

The woman placed her hands on her hips.

"Blue Surf? I've seen the sign," the younger woman chimed in, remembering. "It's close to us."

"Take it with you. I'll come by sometime to pick it up."

"It's better if you take it now. I'm leaving too."

I sensed where this conversation was heading. I might have been wrong, but it seemed like the mother (as I called her) was looking for an excuse for us to meet again. I didn't want to lead the conversation in front of her daughter, nor did I want to meet her. I came here to write, and already I was entangled with two women and showing interest in a third. Each of them demanded time. What did these women see in me? None offered an answer, and I couldn't find one in the mirror either.

The ladies packed up the umbrella and left. The younger one still looked at me with disdain, while the older didn't glance back. Soon, they would forget me. But I wouldn't forget this beach visit. My entire abdomen was red and hurt more than the scratches on my back.

14

I passed by my favorite supermarket, perhaps the only one in town. I always managed to hit the hours when it was filled with tourists, youngsters, and all sorts of lost souls like myself. Red wine from 2015, some snacks, cigarettes, and something sweet. It was time to get back to my responsibilities and leave behind adventures like last night's. As usual, I stopped at the supermarket's entrance and lit a cigarette. The last time I did this, Maria appeared out of nowhere, sparking my interest for the first time, even though I had known her before that. I didn't like women in formal attire like shirts and blazers. It took away their femininity, especially if they wore pants instead of a tight black skirt. Actually, if the black skirt was paired with a very tight white shirt and necessarily large breasts, I might agree. But no blazers, please.

Next to me, a gentleman was doing the same. Smoking a cigarette, looking ahead, clearly enjoying life. But was he also thinking about tight skirts and large breasts? Most likely. We're men. 90% of the time, we only think about breasts and butts. In the remaining 10%, we think about how to get to them. Men are simple creatures, and I didn't want to change anything about us.

I crushed my cigarette in one of the bins and headed towards the hotel. Along the way, Denis called me.

"They're waiting for my response about the screenplay."

"Great. What should I do?"

"Idiot. I've been waiting for a response from you for two days. Am I supposed to write it?"

"It's ready."

"Really?" I could sense his happiness just from his voice over the phone.

"I'm kidding, agent. Of course, accept it. We'll make good money."

"I want you to be serious. You've never written a screenplay before. Do some research on how it's done."

"Easy. Take the text and divide it. Simple work for a few hours."

"It seems to me you're taking this whole thing as a joke. Get serious, Alex."

"Don't worry, buddy. Everything will be fine."

I hung up. I really had no idea how to write a screenplay, but I assumed it was something close to what I told Denis. I had the text. What more did I need to add? My mind was elsewhere. And no, it wasn't on Olga or Lora. Though I wished it were. My mind was on the new book. My muse had struck me at the most opportune moment. I couldn't wait to sit down and write.

As I passed by my sedan, I kicked its tire. Just so it knew who's boss. If this screenplay thing worked out, I'd buy a new car to neglect in the same manner. Whoever said cars attract women hadn't seen me. This wreck had been the scene of sin for not one or two women. Yes, some of them, when we argued later, said I drove a clunker, but how can you insult someone by telling them the truth?

The reception was empty. So was the foyer before it. I bypassed them and went up. On the stairs, I passed one of the elderly couples I had seen checking in earlier. They greeted me, and I returned the gesture. When you're old, you greet more often. Perhaps it somehow scratches your ego and deludes you into thinking you're still young and that the youth considers you part of society. Young people don't greet each other. If two men meet eye to eye, usually a hostile thought and envy pass through their minds. They weigh with their eyes who is stronger and who has more money. At least that's how it is now. But if a strange woman and man lock eyes, it's always about sex. Even if it never happens and even if there's never hope for one of them. Both subconsciously think about sex.

And in most cases, the man has already bragged that she's his next conquest. And she's never even seen him.

I entered, locked the door, stood under the warm shower for a while. And as usual, the best ideas come either under the shower or over the toilet bowl. I wanted to buy a motorcycle. Just leave my car here to fate and leave on a bike.

When I came out, the laptop was already waiting for me on the terrace, the sweets were opened, and so was the wine. Across, two women were chatting on their terraces in swimsuits. What more could a 35-year-old man want?

<h1 style="text-align:center">15</h1>

I wrote again until morning. Some of the world's best and most famous authors forbid incorporating personal experiences into books, but I couldn't resist. My experience with Olga could easily translate into the story of the boy in love with his beloved's mother. Every time I write or mention this, I laugh. But such things exist, not just in my book or in porn. They're part of the real world too.

I didn't see Olga as a mother, but the sex with her was fitting. The first two times, I finished as quickly as a boy tasting the kisses of love for the first time, especially with an older woman. We've all been with such women and know it's somehow more memorable. The boy finished on the first thrust. But unlike with his beloved's mother, no wine bottle fell. No glass broke. The mother laughed on his shoulder, just like Olga did on mine. But the boy's beloved's mother was probably expecting it, while Olga and I did not. Though our earlier passion might have hinted at it.

I described the second attempt too. It was more successful for the boy. Having gone through the trial of the first time, he lasted longer the second time around. However, I didn't succeed with Olga. Well, she was a passionate woman. While the boy didn't understand passion. He just wanted to touch the most precious part of his beloved's mother. Hands-free.

The text flowed so smoothly it seemed to write itself. I wouldn't be lying if I said it felt like it was writing itself, and I was just watching from the sidelines. And I felt the emotions that the inexperienced boy and the mother of his beloved were feeling. It sounds exactly like a plot from a porn movie, but it's not. By morning, I had gotten aroused twice, which subsided on its own. I wasn't sure if it was because of what I was writing or my memories with Olga. God, if I didn't manage to hook up with the neighbor before she left, I'd go back and do it again with Olga.

Morning again caught me shirtless, in shorts, and white socks. But this time, I wasn't in the bed of a blond beauty; I was in front of my laptop, finishing page fourteen. Four more than my usual. The story continued two days after the boy's first time. He talked to the one he loved. She had become a bit kinder to him. But he seemed to think more about her mother. Or just couldn't get her mother out of his head. The boy was confused but satisfied. He tried to deal with his inner demons. But he didn't yet know what awaited him. Soon, his beloved's sister would want the same.

I was ready to go to bed when I smelled cigarette smoke. The last cigarette I had smoked was more than an hour ago. The smoke wasn't from me. It was coming from somewhere nearby. I pushed the laptop forward, pushed my chair back, and stood up. It was around 7 AM, my favorite time to go to bed. I leaned on the railing and looked in the direction from where the smoke was coming. My eyes met a blue wave. And the blue wave was in the eyes of Lora. She smiled at me. As if she was waiting. I was slightly surprised. I hadn't realized our terraces were next to each other. I leaned forward and looked behind her. I wanted to make sure the fat man wasn't there.

"Are you checking out my butt?"

"No. I'm checking for danger."

"So, my butt?"

"That too."

"He's not here. They went out for a men's breakfast."

"Why did they leave you behind?"

"They went out for a man's time." She smiled and took another drag of her cigarette.

"So early?"

"Haven't you ever been on a family vacation? You get up early, go to the beach, nap in the afternoon, and after a few beers, you go to bed. And the next day, you do it all over again."

"Sounds awful."

"It's not. At least you're with your loved ones."

"You mean your child?"

She didn't answer. Took a drag and looked ahead. She was wearing a thin, colorful nightgown with sleeves rolled up. I wanted to see the outline of her butt through the nightgown. I would give anything to be behind her at that moment.

"Why are you up so early?"

I reached across the terrace and took the cigarette from her mouth. I took a drag and returned it to her. I didn't really want to smoke, but I wanted to slightly irritate her.

"I write at night and sleep during the day."

"So you've been writing until now?"

"Yes."

"And you've polished off a new bottle?"

I remembered the empty bottles in the room. She had noticed them. How had I forgotten to remove them?

"You could say that. Wine helps with writing."

"Are you famous?"

"If you have to ask, then I'm not."

"I don't read much. I used to when I was younger, but then I discovered boys and books seemed boring."

"That doesn't sound very appealing."

"Well, I've been with my husband since I was sixteen. Twelve years now. How does that sound?"

"Have you had other men while you were with him?"

She looked at the fingers on one hand, folded four of them, and showed me the remaining one, which she wiggled cheerfully.

"Just one? I'll consider that normal."

"As you say. I don't regret it. My husband doesn't satisfy me. Actually, I don't know why I'm sharing this with you."

"Sometimes I have that effect on people. But I can keep a secret. At most, I'll include your story in a book."

"Just change my name."

"Which do you prefer? Iva or Lara?"

"You won't be very smart if you change Lora to Lara. And you promised me the text of your new book. But only if it has sex."

"I'll send it to you on one condition."

She waited for my condition.

"I want you to describe how you felt while reading it. In detail."

I waited for her to go inside first. I tried to see her butt but couldn't. I sat at the laptop, copied the last part I had written that evening, and sent it to the email Lora had left me. I added the empty wine bottle to my collection and went to bed. I stared at the ceiling for a few minutes, trying to hear any noise from the next room, but I couldn't.

16

Something was happening around me. At first, I thought I was dreaming, but then I abruptly opened my eyes and got up. I was certain someone was in the room. I ran all the way to the bathroom. No one was there. I returned and sat on my bed. Whether it was the wine or the stress, something was starting to break me down. I felt like a wreck. And I had come here to rest. Usually, when it got like this, I'd just change cities. But now, there were too many reasons to stay. Yes, the book I was writing was the most important, but Lora intrigued me more. I wanted to see how far things could go with her. Not knowing how much longer she'd be in the hotel, I needed to act fast.

Another reason was Olga. Falling asleep, I thought about her. The sex with her was so good I wanted to repeat it. But it could also be the biggest mistake of my life. We had an understanding that it was just for one night. We didn't say it, but it was implied. And if I just showed up now, I'd look like a pathetic man begging for sex. Or worse... fallen in love. And I hadn't. But did she think of me, as I did of her? I hadn't left in the most gentlemanly manner, but isn't that how lovers part ways? What if she was just sitting somewhere crying over me?

I didn't believe it. I'd probably look for her, but after finishing my other business. Not the book, nor the script.

But Lora.

I got up from the bed and went to the terrace. Only then did I see the time. It was just after 11. I had slept no more than four hours. I wasn't sleepy. While checking my emails and lighting a cigarette, I watched the opposite terraces. My neighbors' towels were gone. It was beach time, and everyone was there. Everyone except wine-loving writers like me. Lora was probably at the beach with the love of her life, whom she had cheated on once. Well, I wouldn't lie if I said I hoped to be the second. Unless she broke up with him before sleeping with me. I hoped that wouldn't happen and she wouldn't do it. And why did I always end up with women with children? I could barely support myself...

My door opened. It was the housekeeper. I felt a déjà vu seeing her.

"Sorry. There was nothing on the door, so I entered."

The woman got scared when she saw me and started backing away.

"It's fine, come in."

She quickly changed the sheets, took the towels, even the one all sandy from the beach. She said nothing. She even pretended not to see the blood on some of the sheets. My back was still bleeding occasionally, staining everything it touched.

"Do you want me to throw these away?" She pointed at the bottles.

"No." Not that I didn't want to. I was just embarrassed by them. "I'm collecting them."

"Okay, then."

She left, and I sat back at the laptop and opened my emails. I hoped for one from Lora, but there wasn't any. I tried to write but couldn't get more than two sentences down. It was hard to write during the day. I put on a shirt and left my room.

"Ah, finally!"

Maria was at the reception. She looked better when I saw her at the supermarket parking lot, but she was still attractive now. Her hair was tied up, and a scar on one side of her face was visible. It didn't make her ugly; it actually added some charm. She seemed to notice me looking at it and looked down.

"Hello."

"Don't you recognize me? Your favorite guest?"

There was something in her eyes. She was sad and scared.

"They don't let me talk to the guests."

"Well, isn't that your job?"

"Yes, but... I've been too personal with them. Don't ask any more."

I didn't ask. I assumed it was because of me. Sometimes I really did go too far. I left her and went out. It was noon, and I was starving. I passed by my sedan outside. It was still there, unfortunately, now adorned with shoe marks and bird droppings. I had neglected it so much. Once upon a time, we were in love.

I crossed the small street in front of my hotel and turned left, passed by the supermarket, and entered a sort of restaurant. I remembered it from the last time I was in town, more than four years ago, with my then-girlfriend.

I considered girlfriends those with whom I had lasted after more than two arguments. And with me, there were always arguments. Initially, I blamed everyone else, but now I knew I was often the reason for them. Her name was Emilia, and she had light blond hair, almost white. I don't know if she dyed her hair, but I rarely saw hair like hers. She was with me even when I took her to low-quality bars like the one I was in now. As an emerging writer, I didn't make much. Initially, I edited various small articles for newspapers and wrote brief reviews of lower division football matches. I earned slightly above the minimum wage for that. At the same time, I learned about drinking and wrote my first book. Luckily, I was in a writers' circle, and one of the higher-ups agreed to edit my book for almost no money. I was fortunate that it somehow became popular. Well, not for long, but there was a period when I often saw it in book-sharing groups. Some people insulted me for being a big cynic, others were happy for me. I quickly stopped reading both. Honestly, I didn't care what they thought. I just wanted to write what I felt.

Somewhere after this bar where I was now, Emilia and I broke up. Actually, it wasn't the bar's fault, but mine. She caught me texting with one of my colleagues. It was true, but I hadn't slept with her. Just texted. I had slept with another one that Emilia didn't know about. But I accepted her viewpoint. In fact, I included many of our stories with Emilia in my second book. Yes, I again broke the rule of not using personal experiences in writing, but what did it matter if great authors had said it?

I had my own style.

The second book exploded even more. The main character was different, but he also loved alcohol and won cases drunk. The legal profession immediately jumped on me, saying it was impossible to have drunk lawyers. At first, I tried to explain that it was just a book, then I gave up. Let them sue me. I'd hire a drunk lawyer. And now, that joke still made me laugh.

The waitress was young and angry. If she didn't scowl so much, she'd definitely be prettier. I tried not to stare at her. I might have been anything, but I didn't mess with girls under eighteen.

On my plate was a veal steak, some potatoes, and in front of me, a glass of red wine. I loved wine, what could I do? Most of the tables were empty, which was a bit strange for lunchtime in a big resort town, but they slowly started to fill up. I ate slowly and watched the passersby, thinking about the book. The next chapters wouldn't have much development, but I'd flesh out my main character. Did Lora read it? And how would she react? My biggest fear was that she'd leave before we got to know each other.

I paid my bill and went for a walk. I wasn't sleepy or inspired to write. And I didn't even want to think about the beach. I was done with beaching for the year. My chest still hurt from the sunburn.

I reached the bench where I met Olga. It was empty. I sat down and stared at the beach below. Two ladies in swimsuits provocatively passed in front of me. They probably weren't wiggling their butts just for me, but I was grateful for the view.

I watched them as long as I could until a tap on the shoulder snapped me out of the trance my subconscious cells had fallen into.

17

"A thief always returns to the scene of the crime."

The voice was familiar. I turned my head. Tall, blonde, beautiful, in tight jeans, a loose white t-shirt, and hair tied up. It was Olga. Holding my shoulder and with a wide smile, she spun around and sat next to me. For the first time in years, I felt nervousness from being close to a woman. Why did she affect me this way?

"If you're going to kill me, let's not do it in front of so many people."

"Why would I kill you? Wait, is that why you haven't looked for me for so long?"

"Actually, yes. I snuck out not exactly like a gentleman."

"I didn't expect you to be a gentleman. I even hoped you'd be gone when I woke up."

"You didn't have time to hope. You managed to finish three times."

"It was twice, I faked the third."

I pulled out a cigarette and bit it, looking at her. She laughed, leaned close to my ear, and whispered:

"But I admit, I've never had better sex."

She said it, leaning her head close to mine.

"Next time we have to try and last more than a minute."

"If there is a next time." She pulled back slightly.

"Until a moment ago, I was sure there wouldn't be. But now I know I could take you right here."

"You wouldn't dare."

I grabbed my shirt and took it off. I leaned towards her half-naked, and she gasped with laughter, pushing me away with both hands.

"People are watching us."

"You said I wouldn't dare. I love being challenged."

"Put your clothes on. And for God's sake, what happened to your chest?"

"You should see my back..." I turned my back towards her. It must have looked funny because she covered her mouth, trying to stifle her laughter.

"Which cat clawed you like that?"

"A special breed of blonde cat."

"At least you got away with just that. When I woke up, everything around me was covered in blood."

"My blood."

"I slept like a baby. Woke up around noon. And it was the doorbell that woke me."

"Another lover?"

"Stop." Her smile faded. "And which lover would look for me in the afternoon?"

"Well, you're right there. I would come at night. But only if you have wine."

"You didn't come back. But let's leave that aside – a group of tourists was standing at the door. The group I was expecting. Outside, there were eight people, and around me, it looked like a crime scene."

"I told you, you're a predatory breed."

"You didn't say predatory. Just blonde."

"It's almost the same."

"I put on a clean robe and went out. I don't know how I must have looked to them, but initially, they didn't take me very seriously. I offered them a cup of coffee while they waited for their rooms."

"I cleaned the floor. – I tried to highlight my contribution."

"Yes, thank you for that. If they had seen the broken glasses on the floor, they might have left altogether."

"And if you had taken them into the bloody room..."

"The bloody room? Someone might think it's a room where a murder happened."

"Do you want to see my back? It was almost a murder."

"Fortunately," she continued, "all the rooms are booked."

"Unfortunately, we can't go back there."

"Yes. And what about your place?"

"My room is available."

"I'm not asking about your room. I'm asking how you're doing?"

"Oh, you know how it is with writers. Alcohol, writing, alcohol, writing, alcohol, women."

"Women?"

"They're around."

She turned away and fell silent. She played the role of being upset. I teased her on purpose. Though there were indeed other women. Especially Lora. But I hadn't done anything with her. Yet I had the desire.

"And your other two houses?"

"In one of them are my mother and sister with Peter. That's where I sleep, too. The other is rented out to guests."

"So our affair ends here. We should have made love right here on the bench."

She tried to suppress her smile again, unsuccessfully. Covering her mouth with her hand, she turned to me.

"Or you could invite me to your room. Unless you're ashamed of me in front of your other... WOMEN."

She shouted the last word, and I couldn't help but laugh.

"Why didn't you make a fuss about the alcohol? I think drinking is worse than sleeping with women."

"And talking about other women in front of one who is ready to take off your pants any moment isn't the best thing for your life."

"And who would that be?"

"You'll find her in your room tonight. But only if I come, too."

She was too close to my face. I tried not to kiss her, but I couldn't resist. We leaned in, and in a moment, she was on top of me, and we pressed against each other like teenagers who had just discovered kissing and wanted to show it off to the entire town.

18

Olga stood on one of the chairs on my terrace, and I stood next to her. She was resting her head on my shoulder. We hardly spoke. We just looked into the distance, smoked cigarette after cigarette, and kept silent. She had lied about not smoking. Well, she didn't smoke as much as me, but still significantly more than I had expected.

I stroked her hair with my fingers, and she slightly closed her eyes every time I ran my fingers across her temples. She enjoyed it as cats do when you find that perfect spot to pet them.

On the opposite terraces, several women walked around in swimsuits. I watched them, and so did Olga. But now, I really wasn't interested in their behinds. I only wanted Olga's. Yet, the moment wasn't right to move. I could stay like this forever. I hoped I wasn't falling in love. I wanted to forget about Olga, Lora, and everyone I had met here once I left the city, sooner or later. That's how I lived, and I didn't plan to change my lifestyle.

"Do you write here?" Olga whispered softly.

"Yes. All night long."

"It's somehow beautiful. Even though your view is just another concrete hotel. But at least you can watch the nice behinds of the vacationers."

"Almost no one passes by at night. But you're right, I do watch them sometimes."

"You're a man. I didn't expect anything else."

She continued to lie on my shoulder. I liked this. No matter how much of a nonchalant person I was, and how primitively

I sometimes behaved with people, moments like this were irreplaceable, even by the best bestseller. Though, if there were good money in the bestseller, I might take my words back. Anyway, while I was with Olga, I didn't think about anything else. Not even about Lora, who was probably lying next to her fat husband thinking about me. Or about one of her past lovers.

Olga lifted her head and kissed me. I placed my fingers under her chin and lifted it. I pressed my lips to hers, and for a moment, we stayed like that. The taste of her lips was like raspberry, and her breath was of cigarettes. Both flavors intertwined and aroused everything in me. Raspberry was a feminine scent that excited me, and cigarettes carried the scent of carefreeness and easy love. Yes, with Olga, it was easy love. Neither of us had fought for each other. Nor did we know anything about each other. Yet here we were. For the second time, we stood next to each other, and although we hadn't yet consummated our desires this evening, we could drink from our love.

I don't know how long we stayed like that, but when we moved towards the bed, she was hanging on my neck, and I passionately squeezed her behind with both hands. She moaned quietly again. For the first time, I encountered a woman who got aroused so easily. I didn't believe her words that it was only with me like this. I had enough experience to understand when a woman desires a man as she desired me and when a woman lies to a man to keep him with her. I fit into both categories.

This time I didn't throw her. Although I wanted to. The way she moaned in my arms, I wanted to hurt her. But not the kind of hurt where physical pain is the main element. I wanted her to scream in my arms and moan.

I gently placed her down, she wrapped her arms around my neck and pulled me towards her. She didn't want us to rush. I understood that without her saying it. Slowly, I took off her shirt and went down. Holding both sides of her waist, I went lower. I let her go, unbuttoned her jeans, and slid them off. She was now in her underwear and bra. She had stretched her arms up, closed her eyes, and quietly moaned. I moved up and kissed her neck, she grabbed my biceps, small as they were.

I uncovered her breasts and kissed each one. I didn't linger there long. I could feel her excitement through her body. She was trembling. I quickly left her breasts. There was a risk she might climax before we even got to the main act.

Her underwear was already on the floor. God's gift between her legs was wet. Around the sweetness, there were slightly swollen little hairs. I placed my lips and lightly inserted my tongue. She moaned. I pulled my head back, and she grabbed it with both hands, pressing it into her most cherished spot. I took her hands off my head. I tried to look into her eyes, but she wasn't looking. Her eyes were closed, enjoying the moment.

"Put it in."

When a man hears those words, especially with the moaning tone of an excited and naked woman, it can be said he has reached the peak of his sexual prowess. And if the man was the predator and the woman his prey, he had already captured her. He had proven to be stronger and faster than her. And the prey lay in his clutches, awaiting the end of her life. For the predator, it remained to play with her, and when boredom overcame interest, to bite her neck and take the life out of her.

My teeth left a mark on her neck, and the penetration was so sharp that her scream echoed throughout the room, and I was sure it could be heard in all the rooms of the hotel.

19

Did I think about Lora that night? No.

Actually, just once. It was at Olga's first cry of pleasure.

For a moment, I worried that too many people might hear us, but then I felt pleased and satisfied. Let as many people as possible hear what a lover Alex is. I imagined Lora lying next to her bulky husband, both of them had turned their backs on each other, but neither was asleep, listening to Olga screaming all possible vocal sounds, mixed with my name, and sometimes hers. Yes, it was the first time I heard a woman in full ecstasy screaming her own name. It was a kind of self-satisfaction. If I could describe it somehow, the tone was accusatory, and Olga was searching for her morality. Naturally, she didn't find it. And how could she while making all the hotel guests envy her as she broke dozens of God's laws with me?

We did it three more times that night. By the last time, her voice had disappeared, and only some raspy voice of an old drunkard came out of her mouth. With each attempt to speak, we both laughed while our sweaty heads rubbed against each other. The wounds on my back had reopened, and blood was dripping everywhere. I was going to be embarrassed in front of the housekeeper again tomorrow. But I didn't care. I wanted her one more time. But I had no strength left.

The morning found us entwined with each other. Over the years, I had slept with many women, but none of them experienced such pleasure from sex. And usually, when the act with them was over, everyone turned to their side of the bed and ended their day thinking about something or someone else. Even with my two serious relationships, it was like this after the initial saturation with each other. With Olga, it seemed different. She had clung to me like a bear and had fallen asleep that way. The dried sweat on us carried a salty taste in the morning.

We woke up as we had finished. Together. I opened my eyes, and then she did. She kissed me on the lips and looked into my eyes. I think she was in love with me. And I was not in love with her. Or at least I didn't want to be. I kissed her. I melted the salt on her lips and licked it off. She smiled.

"You've ruined my morning for the second time."

"Is that the most romantic thing you could come up with?" She pulled away.

"Darling, I came here to write, not to roll around with blonde temptations."

"Didn't we write enough last night? And the night before. The first time with blood, the second with sweat."

I ran my hand over my back as far as I could reach. I looked at my fingers. There was blood again. She saw it and laughed.

"If you keep fucking me like this, your back wounds will never heal."

"You get aroused too easily," I said. "I've never seen a wetter woman."

"Will you ever stop talking about your other women?"

"Are you jealous? It was supposed to be just for one night."

"And now I've been here for a second."

"By the third, I'll decide you like me."

She grabbed my pillow and threw it at me. Then she buried her face in hers and started to cry softly.

That's how women were. One moment they were in ecstasy and the happiest in the world, and in others, they cried. And when a woman cries, it's one of the nastiest sights a man can encounter. Women didn't deserve to cry. Women only deserved to scream, having reached the breaking point in one of the most primal skills known to man. And with Olga, that was easy. But throughout all this time, I never suspected she could also cry.

I moved closer to her and tried to comfort her, even though I didn't know why she was crying. She turned her head. Her eyes were in tears. I kissed them. She stopped crying, but didn't say anything. I lay down next to her, she moved and climbed on top of me, intertwining her fingers with mine. She started kissing me. I grabbed her waist and moved her aside. I wanted her terribly, but it couldn't always be her way. And to have sex when we just needed to talk. She stayed where I had moved her. She looked at me.

"What's wrong?"

"I think I fell in love."

Just not that.

"With whom?" I couldn't help myself.

"I'm stupid, I know," she ignored my question, which was out of place anyway. "I don't know anything about you."

"But you get soaked every time you think of me."

"Exactly. And you're not even handsome."

That slightly offended me but somewhat confirmed my suspicions about why women liked me. The only explanation was some mystical Cupid flying around me, hitting every woman he met with his love arrow. I wasn't handsome, she was right.

"If you're trying to insult me, you're not succeeding. I know I'm nothing special."

"But there's something about you. You carry freedom."

"They've never called me that before."

"Or maybe you radiate freedom."

"It's getting weirder and weirder. And you're not particularly romantic."

"How do you imagine the future?" Olga lay on her stomach, lifting her head and playing with my face, tracing her finger over it.

"Lots of wine and lots of sex. And here and there a new book."

"And a woman?"

"And at least four children."

"And a woman?" she insisted.

"And a woman. But it's not mandatory."

I couldn't escape myself. I wanted to be utterly honest with her. I had already been burned by baseless promises from me and to me. I didn't want to hurt anyone else. Especially not myself.

"And how do you see my future?"

"Your future? Why don't you tell me?"

"I see myself in a house, on the seashore. With three children running around me and a man who kisses my forehead while I read a book on the porch and drink wine."

"In the part with wine, our stories intersect."

"And in the other part?"

"I don't read books. I just write them."

My answer didn't please her. She turned her back and looked at the ceiling.

I really liked her, and maybe my interest was starting to turn into affection. But affection wasn't love. And I certainly wasn't in love. I was in love with having sex with her, in love with the way she tied her hair, even with her small breasts. I was in love with her moaning during sex.

But was I in love with her?

I ran my fingers between her legs and kissed her. Two of my fingers were already inside her. She moaned. I pulled them out, and she suddenly jumped up and slapped me so hard, a slap I remember to this day.

20

The last part of our encounter passed almost without conversation. I went in to take a shower, and after me, Olga entered as well. Twice I thought about joining her under the shower, but I refrained. The tears in her eyes held me back. I had made many mistakes in my life, especially with women, but now I didn't understand what I had done wrong. I hadn't given empty promises, hadn't promised love, a future, or children. I hadn't given expensive gifts and hopes. I only gave love equal to what I received. And while I thought we were both satisfied with our trade of feelings, it seemed one side had expected something more.

I won't lie. I had those thoughts cross my mind too, but I quickly dismissed them before they could cloud my entire consciousness. Whether I was making the right decision or just rejecting my fate, I didn't know. But my heart tore apart seeing Olga leave the room with tears in her eyes. And even the silent kiss she gave me at the door felt more like a farewell than passion.

I was left alone in my room, sitting on the edge of the bed. Behind me were the crumpled sheets soaked with all sorts of human remnants. I don't know how long I sat there, but it was a long time. It was past 9 o'clock, and I sat staring at the wall, unsure of what to do with my life. And it's not like I didn't have tasks. One of them was waiting for me on the laptop.

A hot day was shaping up today. I put on a shirt to prevent the sun from burning my sunburned chest and sat on the terrace. Today, even during the day, I felt like writing. And I had many ideas for writing. I only missed the wine. But I would catch up on that tonight.

The main character in my book once again tried to confess his love to the girl of his life, but she rejected him again. However, he slept with her mother for the second time. Not that he wanted to, but she somehow deceived him. The sister of his love interest also began to play an increasingly significant role. I would gradually introduce her into the story and just when none of the characters expected it, they would end up in bed with the main character. Let him create a story in his world that he could tell for a long time. And as an author, let me be discussed for years to come. I was trying to make this one of the most scandalous novels ever published. I expected all sorts of rights institutions to come after me. But they wouldn't do anything more than give me publicity.

I got tired of writing in the afternoon. My shirt had stuck to my back, and the neighbors opposite were once again parading their bikini-clad behinds. None of them were to my liking, but they were a free show.

I now had Olga's number, but I was afraid to call or write to her. She hadn't done it either. Had everything between us ended before it even started? I missed her in a strange way. I wanted to feel the tobacco breath masked by the raspberry taste of her lips just one more time.

My phone made a sound, and my heart jumped. Not from fear, but from excitement.

It was an unknown number sending me a message.

"I don't know what excited me more... the boy's sex with his love interest's mother or your girlfriend's screams."

21

"Who is it?"

The number was unknown, but I was certain I knew who it could be.

Lora.

"Guess." Her response came, followed by a picture.

I opened the image. It was her, taking a selfie with her back to the mirror. She wore blue thongs and was looking back at the mirror's reflection, gently turning her gaze towards it. Her back was bare, and on the bed in front of her lay a blue cloak. The bed was large, with two doors visible in the background. The photo was definitely not taken in her hotel room and was old, but not too old, as her face was just as I had seen it a few days ago. And her eyes shone blue.

"Lora?"

"Correct."

"How did you get my number?"

"Are all writers as dumb as you, or just the ones who write non-stop about fucking?"

"Just those of us who write about fucking. The blood doesn't quite reach our upper head."

"I thought as much, Alex," she typed, adding a smiling emoji.

"You know my name?"

"Everything is on the internet... names, addresses, phone numbers, ex-girlfriends. By the way, Emily was very pretty. Were you with her last night?"

"That's none of your business, really."

"It's strange, though. I didn't hear continuous fucking, just screams out of nowhere. Unless you were killing someone. But to do it all night long..."

She was getting too personal. Not that it bothered me much, but I didn't want to talk about me and Olga. So, I got a bit rougher.

"I can't talk about my personal experiences with strangers."

I received three dots in response. I had upset her.

"But I could show you if you really insist," I added.

She put a heart on my last sentence but didn't write anything more. I heard a slight noise from her room. I waited to see if anything would happen, but it didn't. I opened my phone, dialed Olga's number, but didn't call. Instead, I used it to find her profile. There were a few photos uploaded. Two with her sister's child and one of her alone, standing on rocks, photographed from behind by someone. The sea was in front of her. No one had commented on the photo, but around a hundred people had liked it.

I put my phone aside and sat back at my laptop. The afternoon was passing, temperatures were starting to drop, though still above twenty degrees. The neighbors across were drinking some fizzy drinks on their balcony. This time they were more dressed. One of them seemed to be looking at me. I looked back. What's the harm in looking? It seemed like she waved at me, but I wasn't sure and didn't wave back.

Denis had sent me another email. He was a strange man. We had known each other for years, had our phone numbers, and often texted each other. We'd send funny videos, sometimes dirty jokes about other people or mutual acquaintances. Sometimes, when he was drunk, he'd call to curse me out and express how much he regretted working with me. I'd tell him I loved him too. And so, our love flourished. Over time, we became very good friends. But whenever it came to work, he'd either email me or call me from his office phone. I understood him to some extent. He wanted everything to be official and not to mix our friendship with work, but to me, it was funny. I didn't differentiate them. Probably that's why he was the one with the money, and I was the one making it for him.

I opened his email. There was an attachment. I downloaded it, but first, I read the email's text.

"I'm sending you a draft of what the screenplay should look like. Is yours similar? The directors want me to send them some draft. How far have you gotten?"

Naturally, I hadn't gotten anywhere. Women had once again overtaken my world and hindered me. Though, they weren't to blame. If I decided, I could cut off all my contacts right now and finish all my work. But would it be worth it to look back one day and only remember the empty white pages filled with black letters and the faces of annoying agents? No. I preferred to remember only Olga's beautiful breasts.

I replied to him in one sentence:

"Don't worry about anything."

22

As those famous on the internet love to boast about their daily routines, I too had my nightly one. I would head to the supermarket, grab something sweet, cigarettes, and wine, then return home to write. How would my routine look if I filmed it for an internet video? It would start at noon, barely awake, wondering if there's a need to brush my teeth if I did it yesterday. Then, I'd lie in bed, staring at the ceiling, contemplating the nonsense I write for a book and how nobody's going to read it. If I didn't go for a walk in the afternoon, I'd have to film a "shopping day," which would be entirely at the wine stand. And at night, under the gaze of the naked neighbors across, I'd sit and write until morning. No one would watch that. Good thing I didn't do it.

I passed by the reception like a speeding train. I'd either pick up or drop off my key, greet, and vanish. Apparently, I had caused them some kind of problem, though I truly couldn't see how. Initially, I just tried to be friendly.

I lightly kicked my sedan as a reminder that it was still mine. It had gotten even dirtier. The pool across was full again, and some dance music was blaring across the courtyard. In our hotel's yard, two elderly women sat on a bench in the garden, chatting. I felt like I was in the big city. Thank God they weren't in swimsuits. I liked swimsuits, but only on bodies under fifty. And that made me realize how old I was getting. Once, anyone over twenty-five was old to me. Now, my perspective stretched even to fifty. But there was nothing wrong with fifty-year-olds. Especially if you're writing about them in your new novel.

Denis had sent me another email and called a few times. I decided not to let him ruin my mood. I'd deal with him tomorrow. I knew exactly how it would go. He'd give me a hard time, scold me, set conditions, then threaten me. Or maybe he'd threaten first, then the rest. I was in too good a mood for him.

I lay on the bed, waiting for dusk. There was about an hour left until dark. I stared at the ceiling, thinking. Modern folks would say I was visualizing success and trying to manifest it. If that really worked, and thoughts materialized in such a way, every man would wake up to his most deviant fantasies, which, in the best case, would land him in jail. In my case, it would bring Lora and Olga to either side of me. One would be holding that thing of mine, the other gently kissing me.

I shook the thought from my head and sat down at the laptop on the terrace. Somewhere, pleasant music was playing. I guessed it was coming from the floor below. It wasn't intrusive, sounding like some rock ballad, providing a good writing atmosphere. Although I wasn't sure how appropriate it was to write about the troubles of a twenty-year-old young man sleeping with the mother of the girl he wanted to be with. Actually, I didn't encounter them tonight. I gave them a little break. Instead, I took the boy and the girl he liked's sister for a walk. After all, they were best friends, and the sister had a boyfriend. What could possibly happen?

Morning found me on the thirteenth page. Again, I hadn't finished the bottle of wine. I felt I was losing my form. And all night, I hadn't thought about Olga. But I had looked at Lora's photo with her backside a few times. Damn, she had a nice ass. How would it look in front of me, if her body was on all fours, elbows bent? I won't lie, I wanted to find out if it was true that when you stick your thing into the most cherished part of a blue-eyed lady, you can feel the sea tides on your member. It should work. Like the seashell and the sound of the sea.

Speaking of the devil, I received a new message. It was from Lora. I saved her number, and her profile picture appeared. It was her with her husband. How sweet.

I opened the messages, specifically hers. It was a new picture. She had taken it herself. Apparently, she was sitting on the bed, because at the beginning of the photo, you could see her pink, perfectly swollen panties, followed by her white thighs, and on them, a laptop. The text on the laptop was zoomed in to show that it was the one I had written for her. After the image, a winking emoji appeared. I started to type a reply, but saw she was sending something else.

"I came twice by myself. I wonder what it would be like if I wasn't alone."

I wanted to write back, suggesting she try with her husband, but I didn't. I would cut off any branch leading to her. My branch was ready for this monkey. I just waited for her to grab onto it and let go of the more stable one.

"I've drunk enough wine to make you scream, but if I'm sober, you'll get much more."

I received some joyous emojis followed by a message:

"We'll be at the pool across in the afternoon. Bring your swim belt."

It was nearing eight o'clock, and the thirst for sleep overcame me.

23

I woke up to several more missed calls from Denis. It was 14:23. I figured it was time to call him back. Sure, I was unserious, but not to the extent of neglecting him completely.

"End of the line!"

"Good morning to you too."

"What morning, huh? Have you seen the time?"

"People of art wake up around this time."

"Artists may wake up now, but you're not one of them."

"I have two and a half books to my name."

"Yeah, and I've slept with two and a half Miss Worlds. The half was a transvestite."

"At least you're not lying about the transvestite."

There was silence on the other end, and I quietly chuckled. I won't delve into the story because it's not much to tell, and I'd surely embarrass Denis. But I kept it in my arsenal, occasionally bringing it up at important meetings we attended together. He always became furious, his eyes turning red, but the rest of the people laughed, and it quickly broke the ice. Such things happened in those high circles that Denis's mistake with something between a man and a woman for them was just a funny story.

"Listen, you bastard," he was angry again, "You haven't sent me anything. You even stopped replying. Are you writing at all?"

"What does it matter to you?"

"I'm your agent, remember?"

"Yes, the best agent. And I'm your best product."

"From the products that have started to rot. Listen," his voice softened a bit, "Send me something, please. I want to promote you. People need debauchery, sex, kisses, and the other stuff you write. I won't even ask about the screenplay; I know you haven't touched it. I know you too well. But at least send me the new book. Or part of it. I want to try selling you better."

"You might make me a millionaire, and I'll have to buy wine with three strong guys for protection."

"Oh, please. With your silly stories? The only chance you have to become a millionaire is if you die heroically and your work rises above the muck. But then only your mom and dad would enjoy your millions. Unless you've left a kid somewhere in your wandering places."

"I don't have kids. Or at least, as far as I know."

"How many bitches have you fucked there?"

"With last night's or without?"

"Drop it, don't answer."

"One."

"Wow, you've become a complete monk. And you're not writing. Next, you'll tell me you've quit drinking too."

"Every man should have at least one vice in life."

"Yes, that's true. My vice is you. You grow on me like a tumor."

I loved this guy. Only he could curse me out, then express affection, and curse me out again. I could never fully understand his feelings towards me. I assumed it was similar to what everyone feels when their pet cat scratches them. You want to hang it from the balcony and threaten it with the worst words in the world, but the next moment, you're hugging and feeding it again. With my charm and carefree attitude, I was sure to live to 100 years. Unless a nervous lady intervened to kill me. And that was a possibility.

"Will you send me part of your book?"

"Yes. I've already received good reviews for it."

"Reviews? From whom?" He nearly shrieked. "Who did you give it to?"

"A lady. She wanted to read something dirty."

"Why didn't you just fuck her instead of sending our book? What if she publishes it?"

"Our book? It's still mine for now. And don't worry about the first part. I'm waiting for her fat husband to fall asleep, then I'll sneak into her room, crawl under the covers, pull off her wet-from-dreaming-about-me pink panties..."

"Yeah, yeah, stop, stop. I get where you're going. Just make sure her husband doesn't catch you first. Can you imagine the headlines... The famous author Alex Nik beaten by the husband of some woman he was screwing in his bed."

"From an outside perspective, it sounds fantastic."

"You're incorrigible. I'm waiting for an excerpt by the end of the day. And tell your lady to delete the book file. Send her your thing to entertain herself with while watching it instead of your filthy texts."

"That's actually a great idea. But I'd rather just show it to her."

"If her husband chases you, run fast. That's the best advice I can give you."

"I didn't want her for anything more."

Denis hung up, laughing. I sat down and sent him the first two chapters of the book. Nothing too shocking there. A boy likes a girl, and the girl plays hard to get. Just like every other romantic book. He wouldn't be able to sell much with that part. But it was a chance to see what kind of agent he was.

I had a new mission ahead. I put on my swimsuit, which I hadn't expected to wear again this summer, took the hotel's towel, bit on an unlit cigarette, and stepped out.

The heat was infernal.

24

Just one door separated our hotel's yard from the place with the pool. At the reception, the hefty girl told me I could use the pool there without any issues. The irony was, I was going to create a problem for myself and to solve a dilemma for a woman in distress.

The pool was crowded. People were in the water, but most hid in the shade at the bar, pouring beer after beer. A few ladies passed by me, their buttocks overflowing their expensive swimsuits ordered from fake fashion websites. Their skin tanned to various degrees, the paler ones had bared their upper halves and occupied a sun lounger each, lying on their backs.

I spotted her as soon as I entered. Her husband, who honestly, sprawled on the lounger, didn't seem as fat now. Maybe the narrow hotel corridor somehow made him look plumper, but he was still over a hundred and twenty kilograms. He was half-sitting, arms raised, his phone dwarfed in his hands. His neck bent awkwardly, making his throat seem segmented.

Next to him, on another sun lounger, lay Lora. Wearing sunglasses that hid her beautiful eyes, her black hair spread around her. She was in a blue swimsuit without any additional patterns. One leg was bent at the knee, standing upright, while the other stretched forward. Her nails shone in a similarly blue hue, more glossy than blue.

Their child played between them, and the sun lounger next to Lora was vacant. Whether it was a sign or sheer luck, I was both delighted and slightly apprehensive. Sitting next to Lora was no issue for me, but encountering her husband again after our corridor incident... I wasn't sure I wanted that. But, as they say, beauty demands sacrifices, and in this case, the beauty was Lora's thighs, which I simply wanted to delve into.

I started with a brisk pace, then slowed down. Neither Lora nor her husband saw me. I passed several occupied loungers where young folks slept. Someone jumped into the water, slightly splashing my legs.

Lora saw me first but said nothing. She just slightly lowered her sunglasses and gave me a thin smile. Then she put them back up as if she had never seen me. I saw her head slightly turn to the right. She was checking the lounger next to her. Perhaps she too was pleased it was empty.

I was so captivated by her that I forgot about her husband. And if he hadn't called out, I might have lain down and claimed her right there for all to see. Of course, I'm exaggerating, but I wanted her that much.

"Hey, you."

I turned around, hoping it wouldn't be what I feared. Her husband had thrown his phone on the lounger and was trying to stand up quickly, a task he found difficult and somewhat comical. I waited for him to stand. He was at least a head taller than me. He raised his hand with an open palm towards me.

"I want to apologize for the other day. I was wrong."

That was the last thing I expected. The last time this man stood like this in front of me, he was a hand's breadth away from ripping out my throat and eating it. Or at least, that's how I imagined it might go down. And now he was asking for forgiveness. Who was I to deny it?

"Don't worry, it's forgotten."

"I'm not usually explosive, but I don't know what came over me. The maid had overstepped her bounds..."

"Don't worry," I repeated. "No problems."

"I'm relieved, honestly. I hate arguing with strangers. Let me buy you something. Beer? Whiskey? What do you drink?"

"Wine, but only when I write. Otherwise, no."

"Oh, a writer? My wife has started reading lately. Strange business, I tell you. Never saw her read before. Some author, but I can't remember his name," he turned to her hoping for help with the writer's name. She barely contained her smile, her glance at me was mocking, "Anyway. Sit there," he pointed to the lounger I had been heading towards. "I won't bother you. If you order anything, it's on me."

In fairy tales, this was called inviting the wolf into the sheep pen. In this case, the sheep was one, and it would remain with the shepherd, but I would make her think of the wolf even after he had gone.

I sat on the lounger. Lora turned to me and smiled. It had been a long time since I had declared how much I loved smiles. Her husband first watched me for a few seconds, then grabbed his phone again and started browsing. Their little son wandered between us.

I stayed like that for probably half an hour. I wasn't much for pools. Neither liked going nor had gone much. I knew only that the sun began to roast me again. But while previously it didn't work out, this time it was a matter of time.

Lora saved me from boredom. She said something to her husband, then slowly rose from her lounger and headed to the pool. Her blue swimsuit tightened and gently entered between her buttocks as she walked. It was no more than five steps to the pool, but throughout them, Lora gently swayed her hips.

And she wasn't doing it for her husband.

This was one of the hardest moments of my life. I tried to trace every crease of her skin from behind while ensuring her husband didn't notice my gaze. But which man could resist such a view? Even if there was no chance with the girl he lusted after.

Lora sat on the pool's edge and dipped a leg in. I would give anything to be next to her now, to embrace her with one arm while the other ran from her knee to the spot her swimsuit covered. Both her hands grabbed the pool's edge, she slightly pushed off and entered the water. She stayed there with her back to us, then turned, rested her arms on the pool's edge, and looked at us.

Her black sunglasses obstructed whether she was looking at me, her child, or her hefty partner. But I could guess. She stayed like that for a long time, and I tried not to meet her gaze. Every time I saw her posture and remembered her toned buttocks, my swimsuit became increasingly tighter, not a pleasant situation when surrounded by hundreds of people, especially when the husband of the woman making me feel this way was just a few meters away.

Lora exited the pool via the stairs on the side. Water dripped from her. I was going mad watching her. Maybe my desire for her started a little above the navel and reached the tip of my male organ. Sometimes even the inner parts of my thighs tingled. Usually, a beautiful woman, undoubtedly as she was, didn't affect me this way. Yes, I would look, but no more than that. But when I knew something would undoubtedly happen, my appetite sharpened.

Lora didn't come towards us. She walked around the pool, swaying in a light rhythm, passed the bar, and entered somewhere behind it. Not wanting to appear too suspicious, I waited two minutes, hoping she wouldn't return by then. I got up and walked around the pool's outer part, pretending to head to the bar. After standing there for no more than a minute, I slipped away in the direction she had gone. It turned out to be the bathrooms.

Two women entered the women's bathroom before me. I had to enter the men's. The floor in the men's room was greasy and wet. The dirty footprints of those entering had made marks. It didn't smell bad as I had expected, but it wasn't among the cleanest bathrooms one might hope for. There were four urinals and three stalls. Two were vacant, and one was occupied. Since I was there, I used one of the urinals to do my business.

The doors to each stall had enough gap at the bottom typically seen to allow someone to crawl out in case they got trapped or fainted inside. However, through the gap under the door, I saw feet that were definitely not male. They were adorned with not quite blue, but shiny nail polish. I lightly pushed the stall door. It was unlocked. Pushing it more firmly, I opened it.

Lora was inside, leaning against the wall of the stall, one leg bent, the other extended just as she had been on the sun lounger. She looked at me as if the most natural thing in the world was for another person to enter a bathroom stall. I closed the door behind me, and it didn't take long for her to press against me, placing her hands behind my neck, and began to draw everything she could from my mouth. All the blood in my body rushed to one place. She felt it too and occasionally rubbed against it in different directions. I had never been satisfied just with the abdomen before.

Lora was silent. She worked with her mouth. After kissing me a few times on the chest, making me feel like her lover, she then sat on the closed toilet lid. She pulled down my swimsuit and without much delay, took my eager friend into her mouth. Her tongue moved in the same rhythm she swayed her hips walking by the pool earlier. After one, two, three head movements...

She stopped.

I looked at her with the most pitiful expression I've ever given a woman. I looked at her like a puppy barking at its mother, trying to wean it off because it's grown too big.

Lora readjusted my swimsuit, stood up, kissed me on the cheek, and whispered softly:

"If you want to know how my story continues, I'll be waiting in your room..."

25

Women might not understand, but men will surely feel my pain. Imagine standing in a public place with a full erection, unable to move or hide it. It wasn't just my unnaturally protruding swimsuit that was the problem, but also the pulsating pain that seemed to slowly kill me. Lora had completely surrendered to me, igniting a desire within me that was even more intense than before, when she simply walked in front of me, swaying her sweet ass. If I ever became a commander-in-chief, I would decree that such torture be punishable by law.

I'm not sure how long I stood in the bathroom. It felt like hours, but it certainly wasn't more than two or three minutes. Once my arousal subsided, I left and first passed by the sun lounger where I had been lying. Lora was nowhere to be seen. I didn't even want to look the fat man in the eyes, feeling a wave of shame. However, he paid me no mind, continuing to fiddle with his phone.

I sat on the lounger for a bit, then stood up. I didn't want to keep her waiting. Her husband glanced at me. I felt as though "I'm going to fuck your wife" was written on my forehead. I nodded at him, and he smiled back. Apparently, all was well. I walked slowly past the sun loungers and, upon passing through the gate of the veranda, I quickened my pace.

I sped through the reception, climbed the stairs to the second floor, and was hit by her scent. It smelled of lavender. The sensation drove me wild, and the tension in my pants rose again. She wasn't in the corridor, so I first entered my room. I planned to call her and write to her. There was a chance all this was a trap and she had left me aroused, in the middle of the hotel, alone and close to tears. Well, I wouldn't actually cry, but I'd feel like it.

Upon opening the door to my room, the scent of lavender intensified. It could have been coming from outside, or perhaps I had forgotten a bottle of wine open, its scent filling the room as it evaporated. The first thing I saw were two female legs. The second was the polish on her toes. From the corridor of the room, I couldn't see anything above her waist.

I approached slowly and incredulously. Unless I had forgotten a corpse from the night before, there was no chance she could be in my room.

"How did you get in?" I asked.

She laughed. First softly, then louder. She had placed one of her nails between her teeth and clenched it while observing my astonished expression.

I moved closer to the bed with slow steps. My terrace was open. There was a chance she had come from her terrace and jumped over. No, the wall was too protruding. It was possible, but it would have been too risky for a single encounter. I hadn't forgotten to lock the door either. The key was with me.

Seeing her lying on my sheets, which hadn't been changed for three days, her swimsuit had left wet traces on my sheets. She lay there, leaning on one side and smiling. And just a little while ago, that mouth had been passionately licking the firmness beneath my waist, which was now bulging in my swimsuit again.

I didn't care how she got in. I took off my swimsuit and lay on top of her. With my hands, I pulled down the top part of her swimsuit, which remained fastened but now acted as a belt around her chest. Her breasts spread out across her body. She grabbed my head and pushed me downward. I quickly descended, removed the bottom part of her swimsuit as well, and buried my face in the spot I had been dreaming of diving into for days. She didn't moan like Olga, but I felt the muscles of her thighs tremble.

I felt slightly misled. I had expected her to finish the job she had started earlier in the pool bathroom, but instead, I was the one satisfying her. She had deceived me again. Yet the convulsions she experienced with every touch of my tongue made me feel like the best handyman in the hotel.

Like those ads offering their services to fill any kind of holes, I was filling the absence of a man in the lives of unfortunate ladies.

My face was now fully drenched in the fluids from her body, and she was writhing and kicking but not climaxing. I lifted my head and looked at her. She tried with her hands to bury my face there again, but I resisted. I placed my knees on either side of her and, moving on my knees towards her, brought my member close to her mouth. She did not appreciate this. She sat up on her elbows, gave me a slight push so I'd fall on my back, slipped out from under me, and approached me:

"Don't treat me like a whore. This is your first warning."

I admit I got carried away, and it was too much on my part. But seeing her so serious for the first time aroused me even more. I didn't know authoritative women affected me like this. She grabbed my member and proceeded to finish what she had started earlier in the pool's public toilet.

Now on the bed, it wasn't as effective as it had been in the public toilet at the pool. She sensed that I wasn't feeling much pleasure, despite performing some of the best oral magic any woman had done for me. She released her mouth and looked up. For a moment, I read uncertainty in her eyes. I grabbed her chin with two fingers and turned her towards me. I started kissing her below and around the mouth while with my other hand, I stimulated the bud above her vertical slit. She began to tremble again. I lay down, and she climbed on top of me.

"I want you to be a bit rougher," she said, a note of enjoyment in her voice.

While with Olga, there was no need for words; everything just happened. Here, some adjustments and agreements were necessary. This was entirely normal. The abnormal and ultimate experience was with Olga. We never talked during sex, and each of us took full pleasure.

Lora wanted me to be rough, and she was going to get it. I turned her onto her stomach, she put the right side of her face on the pillow and smiled slightly. I placed my hand on her neck in a way that wouldn't hurt her, slightly spread her legs, and tried to make my first penetration as strong as possible, hoping she would one day tell her friends about me. I'm not sure if I succeeded, but she finally made a sound indicating she was enjoying it.

At this stage, with Olga, we usually would have finished and been preparing for a second round. Not that sex with Lora was bad, quite the contrary, we both had fun and stripped away layer after layer of each other's passion. But I wasn't feeling what I felt with Olga. With Olga, sex was like drug addiction. We used each other to experience the greatest ecstasy, then lay next to each other, our brains full of dopamine.

With Lora, we were having fun with sex. Although the more I penetrated her, the more she wanted me. She managed to climax twice and had to finish me off with her mouth. It was ironic. Lora finished what she had started in the public toilet at the pool.

She lay on her back, naked and spread out on my bed. She asked for a cigarette, and I gave her one. She smoked and stared at the ceiling. I did the same, though I began to feel anxious because we had lingered quite a bit, and her husband would likely start looking for her. I spared her that concern. After longing for her for so long, I didn't want to rush her now.

"Did you notice how the girls at the reception have become colder towards you?" she asked.

"Yes," I looked at her, "How do you know?"

"And did you realize that you accused Maria of entering your room?"

"You're scaring me."

"And the fact that my husband argues with the maids isn't a coincidence either."

"You mean to say that...?"

She took a drag of her cigarette, watching my reaction.

"My husband owns the hotel. Actually, he owns several hotels along the coast. We switch between them frequently during the summer."

I pulled back. There was no way to express how shocked I was.

"Yes. He's the owner, and I'm in charge. The usual things. That's how I got in here. I have keys to every room."

I took the cigarette from her hand and took a strong drag. She laughed.

"I don't know what to say." I genuinely didn't.

"Don't say anything. Just enjoy the moment. Because there won't be another one."

"That's what I assumed. At least now you can raise two fingers when the next one asks how many times you've cheated on your husband."

"Actually, I'll still be raising just one." She leaned towards me and kissed me on the lips – "That one was you. I was sure I'd score with the cute writer from the next room."

"How sweet of you."

She laughed again and lay back down. She was wrong to think there wouldn't be another time. Shortly afterward, we had sex one more time under the shower. As we pressed against each other for the last time amidst the steam of the running shower, I realized that I loved Olga. Yes, I know how it sounds, but as I've told you, with Lora it was fun, with Olga it was passion.

26

The evening after my affair with Lora, I stayed in my room. I wrote until morning, although my writing wasn't particularly productive. Until I started drinking the wine, I thought of Lora, with only her wet hair, which had clung around my thighs, and her blue eyes, which occasionally looked at me, in my mind. When I began to drink, I forgot about Lora and only thought of Olga.

And so it went until morning.

When you write about love and especially about sexual attraction between two people, you either have to have lived it or not felt it for a long time. Only then can you have the eagerness and muse to recreate something so personal between two people and make it come alive in the book. That's why the book wasn't going well. Lora had drained from me everything I imagined about sex. And Olga had captured my attention. Sometimes I sounded like someone facing a choice, but I really wasn't. I wanted Olga. And probably, Lora and I would never see each other again. Although I would give anything to see the reaction of the next person she decides to sleep with behind her husband's back and his look when he raises a finger to show that so far, she has only cheated once. The boy would wonder who this lucky person was, just as I wondered what Lora's hefty husband did to deserve sleeping next to such a beauty.

Lora and I were not meant for each other. Yes, the sex was good, but it was one of those acts that would be great the first, second, maybe even the third time. After that, she would start leaning on terraces, smoking cigarettes, and looking for the next one. And I would be in some hotel room enjoying a woman who truly wanted me as much as Lora wanted me the first and last time.

I had written only seven pages that evening. For the rest of the time, I blankly stared into the night. Across, the lights of the hotel sometimes came on, sometimes went off. Morning came unnoticed, the wine was again halved, and I already imagined the scolding Denis would give me next time.

I expected the maid to pass by any moment and couldn't wait to sleep after her. Just as I thought it, someone knocked. I dragged myself to the door and opened it. I cannot tell you the horror I felt when I saw Lora's hefty husband. I tried to remember some prayer because that was my only salvation at the moment. Lora stood behind him, wearing her pool glasses. She held their son's hand. She was smiling. What calmed me was that the hefty man was also smiling. And in his hands, he held a colorful cardboard bag, the kind you give a gift in.

"This is to apologize." He handed it to me. "I told you I'd make it up to you."

There was no need for gifts. There could hardly be a gift that would surpass the precious gift of his wife, which was between her legs. And that gift I had already held. Well, with my mouth. Naturally, I didn't tell him that.

"There was no need. We are men. It's all in the past."

The hefty man extended his hand and patted me on the shoulder.

"We are leaving. I hope you enjoy your stay here."

"For a better place, I couldn't have hoped."

Lora, standing behind him, coughed quietly. The hefty man laughed and walked down the corridor. Lora and the little one followed him. She was in short, snug denim shorts that shaped her buttocks and ended right where her thigh began. Again, she swayed it provocatively. She turned and waved lightly at me.

That was the last time I saw her alive, although she visited my dreams a few more times until the end of the summer.

27

The days following my love affair with Lora, I dedicated myself to writing. During the day, I wrote the script for the series; at night, I worked on my third book. I was nearing the end of my second week at the hotel. Since Lora had left, I had barely gone out, only stepping out to shop, mainly for wine and some food. I reduced my cigarette and sweets consumption, but I couldn't cut down on the wine. I returned to my norm of at least one bottle every evening.

By the end of July, the evenings became a bit cooler, and sometimes I wrote inside, lying on the bed. At least now my sheets remained dry and clean. I wasn't complaining; after all, I had come here to write. And I was writing. Finally, I learned the name of the maid. Her name was Selina, named after her grandmother Selena. I'm not sure why she told me this, but it seemed good to know. She had been working for the hefty gentleman for over four years, yet she didn't know his name. I told her I simply called him "the hefty one," and she laughed. She confessed that my sheets had been a mess the first few nights, but now it was better. How could I tell her that, during those nights, two of the most beautiful women I had ever lain with had passed through my bed? It would have been an insult if she had told me I kept it clean.

I thought of Olga. Even every day. Sometimes I wondered if she thought of me. Several times I reached for my phone to call or write to her, but I never did. I almost forgot about Lora. Once I received a picture from her. It was a picture of the sunset. The sunset was beautiful, but I would have preferred a picture of her sweet backside. I didn't respond, and she didn't write to me anymore.

One evening, after a long session of writing and not so much drinking, I decided to take a walk. The air seemed pleasant and fresh for a stroll. A new girl was working at the reception. I greeted her and went out. I calmly passed by my sedan. I hadn't unlocked it for about ten days. In recent days, the thought of a motorcycle increasingly blossomed in my head. What more did I need? I didn't have much luggage, and I would continue to wander the world as I knew. With a motorcycle, a few t-shirts, and a laptop on my back.

I passed by the bench where I had met Olga. Secretly, I hoped she would be there, but she wasn't. A few children were playing around it. None of them was her child. I went down to the beach and stepped onto the sand. The sand had begun to cool, but there were still people on the beach. Some of them were probably there since morning. I couldn't understand how people found beauty in spending the whole day on the sand and wasting time watching the sea.

The water washed over my feet, and the cold from it began to rise up and stopped somewhere around my knees. I walked slowly along the shore. The sunset made the sea appear red. I looked down at my feet and imagined that the sea was wine, and the wine was licking my legs. I lifted my gaze towards the setting sun. They say that God could turn water into wine. The sun did the same. And when it set shortly after, the wine waves would turn black. And the water would not taste of wine, nor had it ever been wine. It was all a play of light with the eyes of people. Just as likely as the Almighty had done. And just as

I wanted to believe that the sea was made of wine, so did the faithful see the wine in the hands of the Lord.

But who am I not to believe?

28

"Hello, Alex?"

It was Denis on the phone. I had sent him a draft of the script and a few more chapters from the new novel in the past few days. I also told him about the plot of the novel. Naturally, he was shocked. But he was used to it.

"On the phone."

"It's always an honor for me when you pick up on the first try."

"I'm a new person now, Denis."

"Tell that to someone else."

"Are we going to talk business, or did you call to check up on me?"

"I don't care how you are," I loved straightforward people. "Listen, I don't know how you do it, but the script is more than I expected."

"More than you expected? Do you doubt me?"

"I always doubt you. Your brain can simultaneously write the greatest thing in the world, and at the next moment, just erase it because, just because. Doubt isn't even the right word. You scare me."

"What's wrong with the script?"

"You don't get it. The script is fantastic. The directors or the main scriptwriters... well, those who are involved with the series have almost no complaints."

"Almost?"

"I've sent you what needs to be tweaked. It's not something that will take a lot of your time."

"The script is one of the most boring things I've written. At least, are the actresses sexy?"

"I don't know. I'm a literary agent, not a pimp."

"If I were you..."

"Yes, yes, I know. Stop boasting and check if you've received my email?"

They wanted me to change a few lines of the characters. Honestly, I preferred my version, but indeed, the work wasn't something that would take up much of my time. If I got to it tonight, it would be done by morning.

"Alex?" I heard Denis's voice again. "And about the book..."

I tensed up, even expecting him to start cursing me as he knew how. While the previous two issues were about drinking and a few infidelities, now it was about a twenty-year-old boy seriously getting involved with the family of the girl he liked. Literally getting involved.

"We're going to have a problem with advertising."

His tone was calm.

"Meaning?"

"The publishers liked it. The editors too, although they see quite a few problems in the text."

"Problems?"

"They want the vulgar expressions removed."

"So, replace 'sex' with 'love'?"

"No. They want you to replace 'I fucked her mother' with 'I slept with her mother'. I think it's understandable even without the editors having to tell you."

"Everyone has become so sensitive these days. Back in the day..."

"Back in the day? You've been writing for five years. Anyway, I liked it. Your brain is definitely sick to come up with such plots."

"Well, I can't boast about anything other than my plots. And they seem to sell."

"They do sell. The publishing house assured me this one would also be successful. But they won't advertise it in the major mainstream media. Nor will they invite you for interviews."

"Even better."

"I can arrange a few appearances on YouTube podcasts or something similar."

"That's also an option."

Honestly, I wasn't listening. I was just waiting for him to hang up.

"And Alex..."

"Yes?"

"Check your account. The first installment for the script has been transferred."

"How much?"

"You'll be more than pleased. And if you manage to edit it on time, there will be at least that much again. And that's without the bonuses."

Denis hung up. It was typical of his style not to say goodbye words. Just the connection ended, and a thin, short signal sounded in my ears.

I opened my bank account. Denis hadn't lied. The money was really good. It would be enough for me to stay here until the end of the summer and to buy a motorcycle. I didn't plan to stay here after the end of the week. So, the motorcycle would help me to catch the waves. Not the wine waves that flooded every page of my new book, but the waves of life.

I went online and looked at used motorcycles. I liked two or three and got in touch with their owners. They said I could come to see them immediately. We agreed that I would visit in the next few days. The good thing was that the motorcycles were nearby. The bad thing was that this purchase would eat up a lot of my money. But who was I saving for, anyway? I had no wife, no children. I needed wine, a warm bed, and, if possible, a woman's leg entwined with mine.

I couldn't resist. I picked up the phone again and dialed Olga. It was spontaneous. She didn't pick up. I opened her profile and wrote to her that I missed her. I felt pathetic and deleted it. Then I wrote to her again.

29

I don't know why I was so sure she would have replied by morning. I wrote all evening, watching the screen with one eye and my phone with the other the whole time. There was nothing from her. Was she now with another man, or just very busy? And if she was with another man, did she give herself to him completely as she did to me? And if she did give herself completely, did she experience the same pleasure we mutually felt when our bodies merged into one?

I tried to banish these thoughts from my mind, yet they invaded my thoughts more fiercely constantly and at every opportune moment. Several times, I stopped writing and just stared at my phone. I was like a teenager who had just learned what it meant to be in love with someone, and the first thing he did was to start pestering the girl he liked. That's how I had harassed Olga. I had been rough with her when she hinted at deepening our relationship. And when the boy realizes he's in a deadlock, as I felt now, he starts to regret his actions and looks for other options. Yes, sometimes it's better to step back and wait for the girl to come back to you on her own. But in this case, if I left here without seeing Olga one more time, I would never see her again. I was sure of it.

I finished the script and corrected everything the editors wanted. I sent it to Denis around 3 AM, and he immediately responded. Obviously, he wasn't asleep either. I wanted to call him and share about Olga, but I would look too pathetic in front of him. Denis was the closest thing to a friend I ever had.

But I had never talked about such topics with him, much less share personal things. He hadn't with me either.

The book was also doing well. The main character had already sorted out both the mother and the sister of his beloved. And just then, his beloved fell in love with him. You might say that only happens in books, but that's not true. Although most stories are exaggerated, if they happen to more than two people, they are true. At least that's how I reasoned.

By morning, I had drained the wine and wanted more. That's when I remembered the gift from Lora's hefty husband. I had left the bag next to the bed and completely forgotten about it. I took it with me to the terrace. Inside were two bottles of wine, both high-class, old, and dark red. I opened one. It smelled of raspberries. Just like Olga's lips. Another irony. However, the bag held something else too. I loosened the handles and reached in with one hand. My fingers found something soft. I grasped it and pulled it out.

Blue panties. If I wasn't mistaken, they were the ones from the photo Lora had sent me while reading a part of my story. They smelled of a woman. If you wonder what a woman smells like, you've obviously slept with too few of them or you're very young. I laughed quietly. It was quite bold on her part. The bag had been in her husband's hands. I snapped them in my hands and sent her the photo. I got no reply. Maybe it was for the best. I crumpled them in my hands and threw them in the trash can along with the wine bag. Lora was a pleasant experience that I would remember one day, when I'm standing on my veranda, watching the sea, and writing my sixtieth novel while wine trickles down my greying mustache.

Of course, I kept the wine from her husband.

And just then, my phone made a sound. The message was from Olga. A tidal wave surged from my stomach, crashed into my throat, then plummeted down again and slapped into my stomach. The confidence I prided myself on vanished in seconds. I didn't even pour a glass of wine; I just lifted the bottle to my lips.

I clicked on her glowing name. The message wasn't long.

"Tonight at our spot. And bring flowers."

30

One of the men selling the motorcycle called me to say he had sold it to his neighbor. I didn't mind. All I could think about was Olga. I thanked him and hung up. Shortly after, the second seller called. He happened to be in town and wanted to meet me tonight. The motorcycle was my ticket to the next city. Like in video games, where you need to find a key to advance to the next level, I was ready to take the motorcycle and blaze my way to whatever destination awaited. I agreed to the meeting, purposely scheduling it just after my rendezvous with Olga. By then, I would have some sense of where things stood.

Whether I slept afterward, I can't say. I remember trying, even drifting off at one point, but I woke up immediately. It might have been for a longer time, but it felt all too brief to me. Several times I reopened Olga's message to assure myself it was from her. I considered myself experienced with women, beyond the age when merely seeing a woman, even liking her, would make me melt and unable to get her out of my mind. I know that's love, but in recent years, I thought love was for the young. Age teaches responsibility and respect, and sex is just the gift you give each other for making it through another day together. But my thoughts on Olga weren't like my thoughts on Lora. Lora was beautiful eyes, a tight backside, juicy breasts, and a perverted mind.

Olga was simply someone I wanted to hug, to feel on my shoulder, and to let our days pass without even speaking. Words were unnecessary when we were together. And then to gently enter her, kiss her neck, for her to moan in her unique way, her legs to tremble, and the night to end in a cloud of pleasure. And then to greet the morning side by side.

I lay there until noon, then got up and went out. I left my key at the reception, where the new girl stopped me.

"Mr. Nick?"

I turned around.

"Your reservation ends at the end of the week."

"Yes. And?"

"Do you want to extend it, or will you be leaving?"

"Why would you think I'd want to extend it?"

"Our manager said you're a writer and likely to stay till the end of summer. I apologize if I've offended you."

"No, no problem. I did have such intentions, but I'll likely be leaving."

I truly thought so. Even though I was meeting Olga tonight and my heart raced all day, I was still a realist. That's why I hated falling in love. Either I had to break her heart or leave with mine broken.

"Alright. Just so you know, if you decide to stay, just tell us a day in advance."

"And pay for my stay as well," I smiled.

"Actually, no. Our boss said to tell you that you owe nothing till the end of summer. Well, if you decide to stay, of course."

I don't know how long I stared at her. It was funny, but I also felt some respect for the place. The hefty man, whose wife I had slept with several times, in all the ways she wanted, had paid for my hotel.

"Excuse me?" The girl couldn't understand why I was laughing. I didn't blame her.

"Sorry. Please thank him for me next time. I'll let you know what I've decided by tomorrow morning."

She smiled and nodded.

The pool across was again full. I would remember it for the one and only half blowjob I had ever received in my life. I felt like I had been stabbed in the stomach. But then I got mine.

I walked around the city. It wasn't very big. I passed through the new part, then the old, circled the market stalls, walked past a few benches. I hadn't slept for over 24 hours, but I wasn't tired, though I probably looked terrible. The sea was calm, people on the beach admired its blue surges and ebbs. Now, looking down from above and thinking of Olga, I somewhat understood what people saw in it. Maybe it calmed their restlessness. They found peace they couldn't find in their lives.

Returning to the hotel, I took all my luggage from the sedan, locked it, and tossed the keys into a ditch next to it.

"Sorry, buddy. Maybe one day I'll come back for you."

I patted it like an old friend and kicked its tire. Not even the alarm went off.

31

She was sitting on our bench, where we first met. Her hair tied back in a ponytail that gently cascaded down her back. Wearing jeans and a pink t-shirt tucked into her jeans, her hands rested on her thighs, her gaze fixed forward. Nearby, children played, but she seemed oblivious to them.

I approached her, casually dressed as I was the day we met, in black shorts that reached just below my knees and a shirt with most of its buttons undone. I've never been good at dressing or matching colors; I simply wore whatever was at hand. No woman had ever turned me away for the color of my clothes or worn-out shoes. I had the money for nicer things, but why spend on clothes when it could go towards fine wine or a gift for a woman you admire?

As I neared the bench, I traced my finger along her neck. She didn't flinch; her skin prickled slightly. I sat beside her, looking in the direction she was – towards the sand, the sea, and beyond that, more sea.

We sat in silence for maybe ten minutes or more. It felt good. We didn't touch or embrace, but we felt each other's presence, calming me in some way.

"Why were you late?"

She spoke flatly, her gaze still fixed ahead, either angry or pretending to be.

"As if I've ever been on time before..."

"And you forgot the flowers again."

I had no excuse. I had opened her message over a hundred times to ensure it was from her and read about the flowers just as many times. And yet, I had forgotten them.

"You reached out to me..." Olga ignored the flowers.

"Yes. And you agreed. We could have never seen each other again."

"I thought of you."

My heart skipped a beat. I too had thought of her, but admitting it was hard. I fell silent.

"And you?"

She insisted.

"Me too," I confessed. "I wrote to forget you." I lied, partly. I slept with Lora to forget her. But she never left my mind, not even for a moment. Then I wrote. But writing didn't help me forget her either.

"Is that what writers do? Write to forget. Retreat into their imaginary worlds and play the hero, while in life, they're cowards."

"Well, not exactly heroes..."

"...cowards in life," she repeated, emphasizing her point.

"Perhaps. Yes, that's true."

She moved closer, resting her head on my shoulder.

"Hug me."

It was a command, and I complied, wrapping my arm around her neck, pulling her towards me gently, my thumb caressing her arm soothingly.

"How far have you gotten with the book?"

"Nearly finished. Did you know I'm also writing a screenplay?"

"A screenplay? For a movie?"

"No, for a series. They're filming it now."

"What's it about?"

"An actor who's lucky in love but not in work."

"And then?"

"He lands a leading role, something he's always dreamed of. But then he's sent to a rehab community."

"And?"

"He meets the love of his life, stops drinking, nails the role, she cheats on him, and he ends up drunk, driving away. The last thing he sees is the sea."

"Does he survive?"

"The author doesn't say."

"So, women are to blame for men's failures again."

"I wouldn't put it that way. More like a woman's love is a man's cure. Without the cure..."

"So, a man fights for the heart of a woman to cure him?"

"Something like that."

"And your book?"

"I told you, it's with the editors."

"Not that one. I mean your personal one, the one we talked about last time."

"It has a great cover and clear messages. The beginning isn't very promising, but it gets dynamic and interesting towards the middle."

"And the end?"

"I don't know how it will end. You could help me write it."

Olga slowly raised her head, her eyes half-closed, and her lips found mine. This time, there was no taste of raspberries or cigarettes, but it made my teeth tingle, and my chin quiver slightly. She felt it, smiled, and kissed me again before laying her head back on my shoulder.

My phone rang. It was the guy with the motorcycle. I put it back in my pocket.

"Who was that?"

"My ticket to the next life."

"A woman?"

"No, a motorcycle."

She looked into my eyes, seeking assurance I wasn't joking.

"Answer it."

"If I do, I'll move on to my next life tomorrow. To a new place, new stories, people, maybe a new woman."

She laid her head back on my shoulder. The phone stopped ringing. My last words didn't anger her as I expected. But I wanted to be honest with her. She deserved it.

"And if it rings again? I've always wanted to ride a motorcycle."

"We could go places you've never been, drink wine, I'll write in the evening, and kiss you awake in the morning. You can smoke on a terrace at noon while I sleep. We'll make love again in the afternoon, and in the evening, go out so people can envy me for the woman I have."

"And when we tire of it?"

"We'll hop on the motorcycle and head to a new place. There, I'll start writing in the morning before you wake up, then we'll go to a park and cuddle like teenagers. Then I'll take you to every restaurant in town. And in the evening, we'll make love until you fall asleep."

"And when we tire of it?"

"We'll get on the motorcycle..."

"And I'll wrap my arms around you, holding on tight because you'll be the only thing keeping me on it."

"And you're the reason I'll keep riding."

The phone rang again. It was the motorcycle guy.

I ignored it and kissed her. She climbed on top of me, holding me tightly.